THE NORTHWOODS READER

Copyright 1977
by Cully Gage
and
Avery Color Studios
AuTrain, Michigan 49806

Written by Cully Gage
Illustrated by Cindi Nowlen
Cover Photo by Norton L. Avery

Library of Congress Card No. 77-73934
ISBN # 0-932212-11-5
First Edition - April 1977
Reprint - 1980, 1982, 1983, 1984, 1986, 1987, 1988,
         1989, 1991

Published by
Avery Color Studios
Au Train, Michigan 49806

CONTENTS

FOREWORD

Just how does a prospective publisher approach a 290 page, untitled, unedited manuscript about life in an isolated Upper Peninsula village at the turn of the century? Being critical is a must and there are dozens of questions to ponder...

Is Cully Gage's work about the people he knew in that place and time unique?

Is it real?

Does it flow?

Are the characters believable?

Are they consistent?

Are their thoughts, actions, words, etc., consistent with those of real people?

Could the events have actually happened as they are portrayed?

Is the language stilted, offensive or overdone?

Is the language characteristic of the times and the people?

Do the stories stand alone?

Do they say something without being preachy, mushy or blatantly prophetic?

That's where I begin. When everyone else leaves the shop for the day, I tuck such a manuscript under one arm with a jumble of other papers and head for home where I can mount a concentrated attack on the thing which some unknown, unseen person has entrusted to me for critical appraisal. I understand the potency of the red pencil. It is a veritable destroyer of text and ego, but it is my job to be ruthless. I will worry about apologies and rejection slips later...

So I read through the pages once, twice, a third time. I look for answers and for errors in detail. I tidy up some misplaced quotation marks, making sure that spoken words are plainly attributed to someone doing the speaking, and I alter a _few_ awkward clauses, transpose some words, change some verb tenses and adjectival endings, and I read for content.

I down another cup of coffee and start back for work early. I want to leave a few chapters with people who can study them and offer an opinion.

I've hardly marked up the manuscript at all.

And I think the stories are fantastic.

And I want to let Cully Gage know that I approve.

And that I'm excited about the book prospects.

And is Cully Gage your real name?

And what about a title?

And we'll need a good artist.

About Cully Gage's book...

It's beautiful: a sensitive, warm, realistic look at and into the lives of those closest to him at the turn of the century.

He's captured the geographic, economic, sociological, psychological forces which shaped the lives of his characters -- his life -- those elements which make people who and what they are. His writing is alive! His characters don't need their actions or existence justified with paragraphs of explanation. They are simply products of the land and the times. They are part of both and were beautifully simple, real, natural people. They are the the kind of characters which are most difficult to portray, but Cully Gage had and he has them down on paper!

The significance then, of Cully Gage's Northwoods Reader---

It portrays people - real people. They live, walk these pages, speak and act as real people speak and act. There is no pretense, no pumped-up morality, no fairy tale ending. Characters simply and believably play out their roles; their lives -- they grow up, grow old, die, vanish, go back to the farm or the cabin in the woods or just board the evening train and leave.

You can laugh at and with them, cry for and with them. You will see yourself or those close to you in every paragraph of every page of every story. "The Reader" is for and about everyone. You can't possibly be old enough to read without finding yourself in here somewhere.

Times, places and faces change. People don't. Their loves, fears, ambitions, desires and loyalties don't. Whether Cully Gage thought about these things as he wrote or captured this feeling of intimacy by accident, I have no way of knowing. That's unimportant. He "captured" people, suspended them in time and space and committed them to paper. They have found their way to these pages where they can go on living and sharing forever. That is what's important!

Here is a great piece of writing. You'll enjoy it.

Tom Avery
Avery Color Studios

INTRODUCTION

Even now Michigan's Upper Peninsula remains a strange land, but when I was a boy during the early years of this century, it was almost like a foreign country.

Bounded on the north by the vast expanse of Lake Superior and on the south by Lake Michigan and the deep forests of Wisconsin, it was about as isolated as any area in the United States. The only roads between towns were parallel wagon ruts threading their ways through dark woods and swamps. We rarely left the confines of our little village except to hunt, fish or work. Our sole contact with the outside world was provided by the railroads, two of which intersected at our forest village. Their presence enabled the village to escape the fate of hundreds of other little towns which took root along the tracks, thrived for a few years and then disappeared without a trace when the pine had been slashed or the mines gave out.

At one time ours had been a flourishing village too, with more than a thousand men working in the iron mines and as many more toiling in the lumber camps. By the time I was born however, the forest had reclaimed all of it except a thin straggle of houses wandering up a long street -- a cluster of houses at the top of the hill, another cluster down in the valley and the railroad between.

In those houses lived some six hundred people: French Canadians, Finns, Indians, Cornish miners and a smattering of representatives of other nationalities. They shared a rough and tough life, always tottering at the bare edge of survival, rarely having more than a "mite of biting money" and always less of the other kind.

The land and forest was our larder, a pantry which far too often became very bare. The harsh environment only served to strengthen our close community ties. When a family hungered or a man got hurt, we took care of our own. We cared for one another, defended each other, relied on each other fiercely.

Still, as tough as it was to survive in that land and time, my memories of the people of our forest village are filled with laughter and appreciation. Perhaps all isolated small towns breed their own species of uniquely odd human beings and perhaps they still exist in our towns and cities but remain hidden because we don't know or particularly care to know each other very well anymore.

In any event, I'm quite certain that our little village contained more interesting characters than I've ever met since. They were unique and if, in presenting their tales, some hint of nostalgia may be discerned, selah, so be it. Life was simpler then.

Cully Gage

THE WOOING

Love came to Jaako Sonninen at exactly 9:15 A.M., Monday, November 3, 1919. It stopped him dead in his tracks like a pole-axed steer.

It happened right beside the middle counter of M.C. Flinn's store where Josette Bourdon, the new clerk, was assembling "Help-Yourselfs," little striped bags of assorted candies that sold for a nickel.

Forgetting the salt blocks he'd come for, the big Finn just stood there, transfixed, face blank, mouth hanging open. Only the deep red flush creeping up past the collar of his lumberjack shirt and into his shock of blonde hair betrayed a life within a body. Churning delight flooded Jaako in waves as he gazed at the tall French-Canadian girl, the loveliest vision of his life.

Josette was not particularly surprised to see her impact. Many men, young and old, had reacted similarly. She was strikingly beautiful as only a young French girl could be. Vivacious too, infectiously gay, and no more able to refrain from flirting than breathing, she fluttered her eyes at Jaako, smiled shyly, wiggled her tail and continued to make up the little bags of candy.

Jaako stood there red and helpless, jaw agape, unable to say a word when Josette asked if she could help him. She finally broke the spell by popping a red peppermint into his open mouth.

Then she burst into giggles and fled. Jaako turned, walking as if in sleep, making his way past the hardware section, the shoes and boots, the ladies garments... He backed out the front door, took one final look, got in his buckboard and drove away.

Down the wire from the screened balcony where that "old miser," M.C. Flinn constantly watched the whole store, came the little cash container to ring the bell at the candy counter. Josette hurried back to find a note saying, "No more of that, young lady, if you want to continue working here. I'm deducting five cents from your pay for that peppermint."

Josette took the yellow pencil from her hair and hurriedly wrote on the back of the note, "Yes, Mr. Flinn. I'm sorry, Mr. Flinn. I promise never to do it again. I'm sorry. I promise."

She put the note back in the cannister, cocked the spring, pulled the lever and sent it winging back up the wire to her unseen boss behind the hole in the grating. She was scared.

Josette had good reason to be afraid. The job at Flinn's store only paid ten dollars a week, but it was her only hope of ever escaping the confines of the little forest village and a life of drudgery that she and her parents had always known.

The Bourdons were "dirt poor" and had been ever since Josette's father, Maxime, got hit in the back by a great chunk of iron ore while working in the mines many years before. Stooped and crippled by the accident, about all he could do was tend the garden, the cow and pig. The little pension of fifteen dollars a month from the mining company could stretch only so far so his wife took in laundry, mainly from the trainmen and section crews.

All her life Josette had known little at home except steam from the copper boilers atop the kitchen stove and the ironing board that was never taken down.

Before she entered primary school, Josette had learned to fold the sheets and shirts that went in the wicker basket she hauled on her sled to the trainmen's bunkhouse. Later, she had been put to scrubbing them on the blue corrugated washboard that leaned against the rim of the wooden tub, her hands and wrists growing red and rough from the harsh brown soap.

With high school came the ironing. It became a daily eternity of sliding the heavy sadirons back and forth, back and forth, winter and summer. Summers were the worst of all with the kitchen range going full blast. When haying time came, Josette almost enjoyed the respite, no matter how her arms ached from swinging the scythe. At least there was sun and air.

Until she entered high school, Josette hadn't really minded the drudgery so much. "You have to eat; you have to work." It was all she'd ever known. But in high school, because she was very bright and always brought home hundreds on her report cards, the teachers had given her books, magazines, catalogues and dreams.

Josette loved high school, the new experiences in learning, new boys to flirt with, new realization that there were other ways to live. The women teachers gave her some of their discarded dresses and showed her how to rip them apart, steam the pleats or wrinkles out, cut needed patterns from newspapers and sew them into colorful garments. There were no more skirts of dyed Gold Medal Flour sacks. Josette bloomed under their attention and the prettier she became, the more her teachers made Josette feel that she was destined for better things.

Occasionally, on an evening when she could escape the kitchen to join her friends down at the depot to "push out" the St. Paul train for Chicago, Josette would ache as she watched the well dressed people in the dining car eating leisurely with silver and porcelain on white linen. A red rose in a vase adorned each table.

With that ache came hope and determination. Somehow, someday, she Josette, would take the train too, away from this grubby little village with its never ending work, work, work. Someday she would go to Chicago or Detroit and if she ever came back it would be with diamonds on her hands and silk on her back. There were golden cities in her dreams.

But when Josette graduated from high school she found herself back in the kitchen, slaving over the tubs and boilers.

College, even Normal School, was out of the question.

Cut off from her beloved teachers with nothing to do but work all day, Josette became sullen and rebellious at home and almost hysterically gay when out with the boys at night, every night, but never all night.

Josette had made up her mind that no boy was going to get her knocked up. She had seen what happened to her older girlfriends. Fun in the haymow and the first thing you know, back in the kitchen! No, no. Not for Josette.

All the boys tried, of course, but Josette was tall and strong as well as pretty. She could fight like a wildcat and did. More than one young man came home from an evening with Josette with his face scratched or a lump on his head from the heel of her shoe. Marriage to any of them was not for her. She was already married to her dreams of escape, her dreams of golden cities and a life of graceful living.

That's why she was so frightened when M.C. Flinn sent her the note in the change cannister. Money was the passport. Josette didn't care how long it took, how long she had to scrimp and save, but one day she would board that train. In the meanwhile she would take what fun she could, flirt with the boys, bedevil them mercilessly, and tease them out of their pants.

Jaako's situation was different. According to our standards he was rich. He had money in the bank - "bank raha" - the Finns called it.

He lived in a fine frame house with long sheds and a huge barn on a 160 acre farm north of town. It was the best land in the area with no stumps or rocks, with rich soil that spilled great windrows of potatoes on the ground every fall. He had enough cows to keep the cream separator busy filling the cream cans he took to the train each morning. All of this, (and the bank money), had come to him when his father died some years before. It had been hard-earned.

Jaako's father, Toivo Sonninen, came to our town straight from the "Old Country" in 1892, with three hundred dollars gold in his breeches.

Not knowing a word of English, he'd stepped off the train and talked his way up the hill street until he found a Finn to steer him to a boarding house. A big man like Jaako and a prodigious worker, Toivo found a job almost immediately, working as a lumberjack for Silverthorne and Company, cutting the virgin pine that covered our country.

Within a year he had learned English, had been promoted to woods-boss and had sent for his wife, Lempi, to join him in "Amerika." Another year passed and he was camp-boss with Lempi doing the cooking for the thirty men working under him.

Four more years and Toivo was riding-boss, running Silverthorne operations in five camps. He and Lempi saved every cent. When the pine began to thin out, Silverthorne and Company went bankrupt and the bank selected Toivo to handle the closing and cleanup.

There was some talk about how Toivo had "screwed the bank good" in the process, that he'd stashed away much of the logging equipment and kept some of the money from the rest he'd sold, but nobody ever proved it. All that was really known was that after the job was done Toivo was able to go into business for himself, first as a logger and then as a jobber, always doing very well and making enough raha to buy a good farm and have a big pile left over in the bank for Jaako and his mother when he died.

But Jaako and the old lady never spent any money either, except to make money. People said they were both "as tight as a whiskey keg," that "they sold their butter and ate pork grease on their bread."

Jaako certainly never went to the saloon on Saturday nights or to dances or even to the pay sauna. On Sunday he went to church. What he bought at Flinn's store he needed. There was no fancy stuff.

Some of the Finn girls did their best to catch him, for besides having money he was big and handsome, but Jaako showed no interest. He did a little logging, "worked the farm good," and stayed with his aging mother - until he fell in love.

Until Josette had popped the peppermint into his open mouth, Jaako had rarely "gone store" more than once a week and then only on Saturdays, like all the other farmers. Now he came every day right after he'd delivered the cream cans to the depot and picked up the mail.

In the beginning, Jaako would ask Mike Salmi to get him a bag of oats or chicken feed before awkwardly sidling up to the candy counter. Once there, he would stand, arms hanging helplessly at his sides, remaining mute until Josette, giggling, asked him to say what he wanted.

Blushing furiously, he could sometimes only point.

She had no mercy.

She'd roll her eyes, turn her seductive smile on him and pretend not to understand.

"What do you want, Jaako?"

The sound of his name on her lips sent a shiver running from his scalp to his heels.

"What do you want, Jaako? Hard candies, licorice, chocolate, Jaako? Molasses kisses, Jaako?" Then she'd giggle.

Finally the big Finn would find tongue. "No, no candy. Two pounds of dried prunes for my mudder dis time."

Sometimes when she handed him the bag and their fingertips touched, Jaako would tremble uncontrollably, trying to haul out the huge roll of bills in his hip pocket to pay her. He always toted a big roll, big enough to "gag a goat." Not ones either, but fives and tens.

So it went, day after day. Hardtack he bought, dried apricots, cookies from the bins, Nabiscos in the box, almost anything from the counters or barrels or boxes or shelves in Josette's domain. Sometimes he even forgot his change. Jaako had it bad.

As weeks passed, Jaako began to suffer less noticeably in his contacts with Josette. One day he greeted her with a real, "Good morning," instead of the usual monosyllables asking for merchandise. She mockingly scolded him.

"Say Good Morning, Josette," she commanded. "Me Josette; you Jaako. You Jaako; me Josette."

He could only grin fatuously, but from then on he found he could talk to her a little more, mainly on safe things like the weather. Every day he bought a little more and stayed a little longer. Josette was amused.

Just before Christmas, Jaako surprised her by asking her to put up a big box of the best candies in the store. When she teasingly asked who it was for, he answered that he had a new girl.

"This present for her for Christmas. You make it good. Kinds candy you like maybe. My girl, she's very pretty. Nice girl too."

It was the longest utterance she had ever heard from the big man. It almost sounded rehearsed. As she assembled and packed the candies, Josette tried repeatedly to find out who the girl was, but Jaako just shook his head, smiling. After he had untied the rawhide from his roll of bills, the roll that always made Josette's eyes stick out, and paid her, Jaako made his move.

He picked up the box, pushed it across the counter and said, "This for you, Josette. You my new girl."

Then he fled and Josette pursued him.

"No, Jaako, no. Take it back. I'm not your girl. I'm nobody's girl. Take it back. Take it back."

But he was out the door and away.

M.C. Flinn descended from his cashier's cage on the balcony. He was a small man with thinning hair and rimless eyeglasses that pinched a pinched nose on a pinched face. As always, he was rubbing his hands.

"Now, young lady, some advice," he said, sucking his teeth at each pause. "Smile at customers. Don't flirt. You and Jaako bad mix. Oil and water, young lady. Finn and French. Good advice. Back to work!" He had seen all and heard all that had transpired from the beginning. Flinn felt that Josette had the makings of a good clerk. She was pleasant and pretty. She was good for business. He didn't want her marrying that big dumb Finn and leaving. He decided to "nip it in the bud."

Before the girl had a chance to reply, Mr. Flinn had returned to his screened box on the second level. Josette was furious all day at both men.

At closing time, 8 P.M., she left to make the long walk down the hill to Frenchtown and home. Jaako was waiting for her with his horse and cutter.

"Josette," he called. "I give you ride home."

She threw the box of candy at his head.

"You big dumb Finlander. I wouldn't ride with you if you had wings!"

She stalked off down the road with the horse and sleigh and Jaako following, single file in the ruts. It was a strange procession there in the dark. Midway down the hill she gave in, climbed in the cutter and laid it to him so he could get it clear. Josette wasn't his girl and never would be. She detested him. The big dumb ox was only half civilized, had been in the woods too long, had hay in his ears and manure on his shoes.

Jaako heard her out, grinning to himself in the darkness, delighted with her fire and spunk, listening to her voice and not to the torrent of her words. He was in complete bliss with Josette beside him under the bearskin rug with the sleighbells going ching-ching-ching. He could wait. She'd get used to it, but Josette was his girl. Let her yak.

The remark about the manure on his shoes filtered through however, and Jaako responded with the old Finnish saying, "Manure on shoes; money in the bank." That set Josette off again, and she flayed him with her tongue all the rest of the way home. Just before she jumped out of the sleigh, Josette slapped Jaako across the face as hard as she could. It was like hitting a chunk of granite and his grin grew broader, remaining that way for days. Jaako had a girl.

The next few weeks were miserable for Josette, but fun for the whole town, as twice a day the housewives peered through their lace curtains to see the procession with Josette struggling up or down the street, (no one ever shovelled their sidewalks in winter) and Jaako's sleigh behind her.

Nasty little boys would run out to offer their advice. "Jump in, Josette. Get a ride, Josette. Jaako won't bite you." Josette countered by getting some of her young men to walk her home from the store, a strategy that Jaako solved by noting who they were and, as soon as was convenient, knocking hell out of them.

Pow! Pow! "Josette my girl," he would say as he looked at them down in the snow. "You stay away. Hear?"

Raoul DuBois, one of those most smitten by Josette's charms, had to be clubbed down three times before he heard, but by the end of the month she was walking alone.

Josette finally gave in. Hoping with sweet reason to do what she could not with rejection, she accepted the rides. Besides, she wasn't having any fun; besides, it was a long cold walk in the winter storms, and besides, Jaako was always bringing her presents. Some of them ludicrous---a big ball of string, fully two feet across, that he'd tied and wound from bits for many years. This too she heaved at his head. But there were also little necklaces and bracelets and bright ribbons in the packages he slipped into her hand every evening. And on her birthday there were three rolls of brightly colored dress cretonne or calico that he had taken the train to Ishpeming to purchase.

On their rides up and down the hill, Josette tried in vain to make the big man understand that she was not for him or he for her.

"I'm Catholic, Jaako, and you're Lutheran. I'm French and you're Finn. We can't ever marry. I'm nineteen and you're twenty-six. You're too old for me. You're a farmer and a logger and will be all your life. Me, I must go to the city as soon as I save up enough, and I got sixty dollars in the sock already."

She told him her dreams of a better life, of the glimpses her teachers and magazines had given her of something other than the little village in the forest.

Jaako listened happily and clucked to the horse. "I got money," he said. "I take you Chicago, Detroit, maybe Niagra Falls even, so you marry me. No hurry. Friends now, OK. Sometimes more later."

He bought her some skis and they travelled cross-country over the back hills and had coffee and korpua together on a Sunday afternoon. He even took her to a dance or two in Le Tour's barn though he wouldn't dance himself and sat glowering at any man with courage enough to take Josette in his arms for a polka or waltz.

As spring approached, Josette began to admit that she was becoming fond of Jaako. He was so good to her, so big and strong and yet so vulnerable and sweet. No matter how mean she was to him, no matter how she bedeviled him, he just smiled. Maybe, just maybe she'd give in. Only once in all that time had he ever made a pass at her, once when his hand sought her leg under the laprobe. She had hit him and scratched him good on the face. It was too difficult to get at her shoe. All Jaako had done was say, "Ah, good. You fine good girl. I know now for sure. I marry you sometime, maybe summer." She told him again that he was just a big stupid, awkward ox.

"Ya," said Jaako. "You my girl."

They were together so often that the town began to talk and sides were chosen as always; Finns against French, along lines of the ancient feud which always seemed to exist in our town. Up to then no intermarriage had ever occurred between the two factions. The Finn girls only dated Finn boys with the French Canadians sticking to themselves as well. Oh, there was Old Hokkinen who had shacked up one winter with the widow Coreau, but he was a bit nuts anyway and that didn't count. He probably did it just to keep himself warm because he hadn't cut enough wood that fall.

Josette and Jaako both felt this growing social disapproval soon enough.

"What you want to go out with that frog for, Jaako? Don't you do it!" said his mother after Untilla, the preacher, had brought the news out to the farm.

"French girls not for Finns. Never go sauna. Just put on more perfume stink. Don't trust frog girls, Jaako. They loose. You find good Finn girl like Aili. Work hard. Many children, boys too. French girls lazy, dirty. You hear? Forget frog girls now."

Jaako just went out to the barn without a word, and the next Sunday when the preacher raised hell about the Pope and the Catholics worshipping idols in their church and incense pots and Saint This and Saint That, Jaako got red under the collar and did not shake hands after the service.

In her turn, Josette got a workout despite her claims that she and Jaako were nothing more than friends.

Once when Jaako came by her whitewashed log house to pick Josette up, old Maxime limped out on the porch with his shotgun and told him never to show his face around there again. He also laid it on the line with Josette. "You bring zat beeg squarehead to my 'ome again an' me I tell you one theeng. You can pack your sack an' hack." Josette's mother pleaded with her not to see Jaako. He would beat her. Finns worked their women to death. They drank without finesse. They were dour and sullen. No gaiety, no civilite. When Josette next went to confession, Father Hassel scolded her and talked of purgatory. Even her Godmother, Tante Moulin, who had always been her confidant, was rejecting. "I would prefer for you an Indian before a Finn, ma fille," she said coldly.

This intense hostility from both sides served only to bring them closer together. Many long talks and hard questions followed.

Yes, Jaako would take instruction.

"Ok. I go your church and see priest and listen hard, but no promise. Ya, you go your church, I go mine, maybe."

"What about children?"

"What about the children?"

"You decide,"

And over and over again. Did Jaako really mean it about taking her to Chicago and Detroit?

"Ya, even get job dere if you want. Sell everyting."

By this time they were kissing and hugging when they were alone, though Josette had to teach him how to do both. Unfortunately, it was hard to be alone. Someone always came by no matter how far Jaako drove down the logging roads, and then the tale always travelled all over town, getting better with each recounting. One Sunday afternoon when they first drove to Wabik and walked down the railroad tracks toward Red Bridge, they were followed by a pack of dirty little kids chanting suggestive rhymes. Jaako wanted to kill them.

Despite the walks and talks and the fun she had teaching Jaako to make love to her, Josette was still far from being absolutely sure she wanted to get married. After all, her money sock was getting bigger each week from the pay she got at the store.

"Not yet," she would tell Jaako whenever he brought up the now frequent topic of marriage.

"Maybe later. I get sick of this little town and want to go see something else. I love you but..."

Such talk always scared Jaako into silence.

Late in May, Josette asked Jaako why he never took her up to see his farm.

"You ashamed maybe?" she teased him. "After all, I should see where you want me to live."

"OK. We go now. All I show you. Everyting." he answered, slapping his horse with the reins.

Though the girl had heard that Jaako's farm was the best in the county, she was unprepared for the sight of the long fields, green with new oats and alfalfa, or the great white barn and the herd of Jersey cows that dotted the landscape behind it. The large house was painted a spotless white. Jaako drove directly to the front door.

"All for you someday, Josette." he said proudly. When they entered, he called, "Aiti, Aiti, (Mother), I bring for you someone to see." There was no answer, nor was there any answer when they went into the kitchen and saw her. The old lady, stiff as an icicle, had turned her face to the wall. Jaako's face turned beet red with fury and he muttered something like "Saatana" under his breath. Then, collecting himself, he turned to Josette and said, "OK, OK. Never mind her. She get over it. We go see barn."

Leaving by the back door, Josette noticed a long line of sheets, curtains, clothes and blankets, fresh washed and hanging still wet. It was a very long line. And when they entered the barn she noticed the long row of "cow holders", the V-shaped yokes that hold the cows' heads when they are being milked.

"How many cows do you have, Jaako?" she asked.

"Maybe twenty five, but only milking fourteen now," he replied.

"Who milks the cows, Jaako?" Josette's voice was very soft.

"Oh, my mudder milks dem, but she's getting to old."

That night Josette emptied her money sock, packed a little bag and caught the train for Detroit. She never came back.

THE CHIVAREE

I don't know if you had a chivaree when you got married. You may be unfamiliar with the custom. In fact, I'm not even certain how chiv-a-ree should be spelled, but that's how it's pronounced. Perhaps it's a French-Canadian word.

Anyway, when a man married in Michigan's Upper Peninsula, he had to save up a little "raha" (the Finnish word for money), for blackmail or endure the miseries of a chivaree.

My father said that when he brought his new bride up to our forest village in 1900, he only had $1.85 left in his pockets. Since a keg of beer cost two dollars and the cigars and candy another buck, they (the men and boys who met them at the train station) took what he had anyway and decided to settle for only half the usual chivaree. That meant they only raised hell outside my parents' new house until 2 A. M.

When I got married some 30 years later, the custom had about died out, but I still got a taste of chivaree despite the effort expended in bringing my young wife to our old hunting cabin, nine miles deep in the forest.

I should have known what was coming when I found our bunk piled high with logs and a dead porcupine stuffed in the oven of the old wood range, but it was still a shock when the damndest caterwalling I'd ever heard rent the silence of midnight. The grown friends of my boyhood pounded on the galvanized iron sheets of the cabin roof. Then they broke in the door and demanded pie and coffee, and a jug, and money.

"Chivaree... Chivaree," they yelled.

With my new bride weeping under the blankets, I gave them five bucks and the only bottle of booze I'd been ambitious enough to lug the nine miles up the woods trail in my packsack. We drank all of it up quickly there by the light of a kerosene lamp while they offered plenty of detailed advice on how to mate thoroughly.

I had known some of them since childhood; others were total strangers, but all of them confessed to having a helluva good time. When they finally left, my bride had only one thing to say: "Take me back to Iowa!"

My tale here however, concerns the chivaree of chivarees; the best - or worst - that ever took place in our village. It lasted for more than a week, night after night. The old men still talk about it as a classic.

On the back road to the abandoned mine lived a widower, Old Man Putinen, and next door to him an old widow named Aili Pesonen. Both were in their sixties and they lived alone in their log houses though they shared the same log barn for their two or three cows.

They had worked out an arrangement whereby Old Man Putinen delivered milk and butter to a small number of customers in town while Aili did the milking and churning. They also had some joint chickens and the old man delivered eggs.

It was a sensible economic arrangement, but it stimulated a lot of gossipy clack about how far the sharing really went. Even the preacher suggested, gently of course, that they might be wise to get married if only to put a stop to all the bad talk.

Aili and Putinen both rejected the outrageous suggestion immediately. They were just friends.

Old Putinen said he didn't believe in all that ceremonial stuff anyway with licenses and everything.

Said he'd never bought a license in his life for hunting or fishing or anything else. Said he'd fathered seven children by his first wife without a license and was damned if he'd start now with all that nonsense.

Besides, he said, he wasn't about to put out any good money on any damned chivaree.

Putinen and Aili were both known for being tight. She reportedly saved her coffee grounds, drying them and putting them back in the can until they were completely blond, even after she shook them.

She wore shoepaks to church and they tell of the time she asked the butcher to cut the cheese with the ham knife: "I dearly love the flavor of ham," she said.

They were both very frugal.

The talking and innuendo continued nevertheless. Their good neighbors made certain they heard the worst of it. One of Aili's married daughters came home to beg her mother to become an honest woman. The preacher prayed obliquely about them in church. The pressure grew.

Finally, Old Putinen was seen taking the afternoon train for Marquette. Aili had boarded the morning train. The rumor spread all over town, they had finally run off to get married.

When they returned on the evening train they were welcomed by a large and motley group, all primed for a chivaree.

Aili and Putinen both denied however, that they had been married. They had just been shopping. He'd bought a new currycomb and some other stuff, which he displayed. She showed the material she'd purchased for a new huivee (a scarf used by old Finnish women to cover their heads). Old Putinen walked up the hill first. Aili lagged many yards behind. No, they weren't married.

No one believed them.

They were just being tight.

OK, they got a chivaree!

That night the men and boys waited until the lights were out in the two log houses before the din began. They banged pots and pans. They yelled and laughed and sang. They made lewd remarks about Old Putinen's sexual prowess on his wedding night. Kids ran their notched spools against the windows and door, making an ungodly racket. All was pandemonium for about an hour, the crowd going from one house to the other, not knowing for sure where the old couple was bedded down.

Finally, since it was very cold, way below zero, the crowd dispersed. The men went to Higley's Saloon to warm their outsides and innards. The kids went home. All vowed to return again the next night.

And they did, night after night in that terribly bitter cold, but always they returned in vain. No matter how hard the men howled or banged on the doors or pounded their cans, no one came out. No one protested. Only the wind howled back.

After a week of this fruitless partying someone devised another tactic. "Smoke 'em out."

A ladder was brought and erected. Large cans were fitted tightly over the chimneys and smoke soon filled Old Putinen's cabin. He didn't emerge.

OK! The buggers were in Aili's house.

The men took the cans over there and swarmed up the ladders again to plug the chimneys. Again smoke filled the house.

Nothing!

The men suddenly became scared. Maybe they'd murdered the old couple with their foolishness!

They broke in the windows and coughed their way through the rooms, frantically searching for the corpses.

No bodies.

No one was in either house.

They went to the barn. There, in the hay beside the cows, all snug under a down-filled comforter, were the two of them, sleeping peacefully.

Old Putinen was awakened and did the speaking through a snag-toothed grin. "You boykas make goot music," he said. "We no married. I jest helping Aili make hay."

FLAME SYMPHONY

I t always seemed that our town had more than its share of assorted nuts, eccentrics and madmen, but perhaps the impression stemmed only from their greater visibility.

In our little village, everyone knew everyone else and everything about everyone else and about everything that had ever happened to them - back through at least three generations.

And so we weren't particularly surprised when, after an apparently normal childhood, Elsa Gustafson suddenly became a rooster at the age of 17, crowing up and down the street at dawn. After all, her grandfather had become Jesus Christ at 62 and a couple of her uncles had been "stashed away" in the State Hospital for the Insane at Newberry. It ran in the family, that's all.

Our town was very tolerant of such deviancy. Unless the mad one presented some real danger to himself or the rest of us, we simply humored and enjoyed his antics. It gave us something to talk about and besides, most of us realized that on sanity's yardstick we each oscillated up and down the scale at times. We were just glad that the yardstick was elastic.

And so, we always enjoyed the news that old Mr. Hokkinen had shot up his outhouse again. He did it twice a year; in the fall when the lake froze over and again in March when it looked as though it would never thaw.

He didn't know why he had to do it.

"Comes over me," he said and that explanation was good enough for us.

The Hokkinens had the "holiest" outhouse in town and the neighbors said that Mrs. Hokkinen used a pail in the woodshed instead of the outhouse at these crucial times of the year, emptying it on the garden. She raised the best strawberries in town! Mr. Hokkinen was harmless though, everybody said.

So was our "Montanna Kid" who became a western cowboy at age 12 and stayed that way the rest of his life even though he never got ten miles away from the village. He was quite a sight as he rode his imaginary horse down the street. Each evening he would bring the family cow home to be milked, twirling his lariat and hooting up a storm. But harmless.

Well, not quite harmless at that, for once, when fending off some invisible enemy with his left arm, the Montana Kid had pulled out a pistol and put a bullet through his own wrist.

"Take that, you dastard!"

My father took the pistol as payment for patching him up and dressing his wound, but that was all.

It was kind of nice to have a real western cowboy from the wide open spaces riding his imaginary horse down the streets of our town. It kept back the fear of the dark encroaching forest that isolated us.

You had to be really howling-mad-dangerous before they sent you to the Newberry Insane Asylum. Most of the eccentrics among us just remained in town, giving us something exciting to talk or laugh about when winter shut us in.

Two of our odd ones, Elly Engstrom, the Norwegian girl, and Carl Anters, our town's mad genius, managed to find in each other the understanding that they got from no one else. How their lives were linked together and later wrenched apart is not a pretty story, but it does illustrate the difference between our tolerance and acceptance, and it sheds some light on that wide gray band that marks the boundary between sanity and madness.

Most people agreed that Elly, her real name was Elin, was warped into her strangeness by an embittered mother after Leif Engstrom, Elly's father, had deserted the family shortly after the girl's birth. He just wandered away and was never heard from again.

There were tough times, but Mrs. Engstrom had weathered them, making a meager living weaving rag rugs and knitting socks and mittens to buy her necessaries. Leif had left behind a good house and barn, a pig, some chickens and a heifer or two. These, along with a large garden and the help of the neighbors, made it possible for the mother and girl to survive. They still had to work terribly hard though.

At night, when all the yellow panes of the windows of the other houses had winked out, the kerosene lamps in the Engstrom house were still burning and you could hear the thump-thump of the loom inside. Even when Elly was a little tyke she always seemed to be working in the garden or going around town begging discarded clothing. Any kind of clothing would do: overalls, rags, flour sacks, anything that could be cut into strips, sewn together and fed into the loom. All of us saved everything we could for the Engstroms. There were no Aid to Dependent Children or Welfare checks in that day, so we brought them fish and game and did what we could. We did our best to take care of our own.

The thing that really set Elly apart from the rest of us though, was her silence. A little girl in school, Elly rarely spoke aloud or even cried with any voice. She whispered or didn't speak at all.

I remember her coming to our back door with a pail of wild strawberries or blueberries she wanted us to buy. She would just stand there, silently holding out the pail, never answering when we asked her how much she wanted and taking whatever we gave her. It was the same when she came to collect the rags for weaving; she'd just hold out the empty clothes basket and wait there with her wide eyes on us and no expression on her little face. Elly never played with the other children after school, perhaps because they used to tease and call her "The Ghost."

A strangeling!

Even when teased, she just looked at her tormentor, a long disturbing look, then quietly disappeared, sneaking off by herself. Her teachers said that Elly understood everything and did very well in her written work even though she wouldn't recite. She quit school in the middle of the fifth grade though, to help out at home, according to her mother's note.

Her nickname, "The Ghost," stuck even after she'd matured, partly because of habit and because she was always pale, but mainly because she was a night walker.

Except for the few stragglers from the saloon downtown or when some school or church doings lasted later than usual, our streets were deserted after ten o'clock. It was bedtime... That was when Elly walked, especially when there was moonlight.

Charley, the night watchman, might meet her anywhere on the streets: uptown, downtown, even "way back Swedetown," walking slowly, smiling her strange smile. When he spoke to her, Elly would smile or nod, then glide off. She had even been seen in some of the surrounding fields at night. "Spooky!" She was so spooky as to be quite safe in her roaming. Not even the horniest French Canadian would have made a grab at "The Ghost."

Elly was 19 when her mother died.

She came to our house early one morning and knocked at the front door.

"Mother sick," she whispered. "Mother sick."

Dad took his bag and went over to find Mrs. Engstrom dead.

After a simple funeral, which was paid for by the village and which Elly didn't attend, my father and mother went over to see the girl.

They found the house filled with flowers. They tried to talk with Elly, but conversation was impossible. Dad finally asked what she would do, now that her mother was gone. Elly just smiled and shook her head.

My mother tried to say the right things, but she got nowhere either. Elly simply didn't respond.

As they left, my dad laid ten dollars on the kitchen table.

When we got up next morning we found a cornucopeia of birchbark filled with snapdragons in the space between the screen and our back door. There was a short note written on the bark:

"Please don't worry. I'll get along. E." And the ten dollar bill was in it too. Dad shrugged helplessly.

After breakfast he went up to the store and told Flinn that in the future he'd pay the difference between what Elly got from the rugs and mittens she sold him and the amount of her monthly bills.

Elly changed a little after her mother's death. Not much, just a little. For one thing, she began to bring us flowers in the daytime: at least once a week and she continued to do so for several years. She did the same for other families which had helped her. Some were wild flowers: arbutus, addertongue, trillium. Others were from her garden, mainly asters and snapdragons.

Elly spent a lot of time in her garden and several people reported hearing her talking aloud and even singing to the flowers.

Elly would sometimes manage a few sentences aloud, though in a very soft voice, when my mother went to see her garden or brought her some small gift; a comb or ribbon or such. Mother had hopes that she might eventually be able to bring Elly out of herself, but she had to confess that the invisible barriers were very very high.

"A strange child. No, a strange young woman now. Maybe only a man can gentle her," mom said.

"Not a chance!" snorted my father. "She's sort of attractive in a pale way, but Elly would scare off any boy even if she weren't so scared of everyone herself. Who'd want to fool around with a night walker who won't talk? No, there isn't a man in town who'd think of it."

My father was wrong.

Even before Elly's mother had died, one of the kids had reportedly seen her up on Mount Baldy at dusk, holding hands with Carl Anters beside a tiny fire. Carl Anters was our village's other night walker, our mad genius and the composer of flame symphonies.

No one knew the story behind Elly's strangeness, but all of us had an explanation for Carl's - "too much old maid aunt and too many brains for his head."

Carl had been orphaned when he was four. "Galloping pneumonia," they said, had killed both his parents. That was why he came to our town to live with our music and art teacher, his aunt, Miss Anters, who took out papers, adopted him, gave him her name and raised him as her own.

Not a good raising, we felt.

She babied him, protected him, controlled his every action something awful. Carl never got a chance to play with the other children. He always had to go straight home after school to practice at the piano. He never had to do chores or even go to the store like the rest of us. His aunt even chopped all the wood. It was a very unhealthy relationship, some thought. Enough to make anyone into a queer duck.

Miss Anters repelled any comment to that affect with a fury which we felt was way out of proportion.

"Carl's a genius," she insisted. "I tell you, a real genius. Just you wait and see and you just keep your nasty thoughts to yourself. I'm going to help my son fulfill himself even if I do have to live with nincompoops in this ignorant hole in the woods. Carl's a genius. He's not like other boys."

It was tough to argue with her on the genius thing. Carl was far and away the brightest student we'd ever had in school. He was reading books and had mastered arithmetic before he entered first grade so they stuck him in the third where he spent the whole year bored silly. He also skipped the fifth grade and the seventh and then finished high school in three years.

All the teachers were delighted to see him go!

Carl wasn't silent like Elly. He talked all the time instead and Carl asked the damndest questions: questions that no teacher could answer without making an absolute fool of herself. Most of us kids couldn't understand

him most of the time anyway because of the big words he used.

I remember feeling a little sorry for Carl once and so I asked if he wanted to go trout fishing with me. He refused.

"Unfortunately, Gage, I have only a miniscule interest in fish of any variety. I have studied something of ichthyology and frankly, the species has little pertinence to my goals."

I never wasted the time feeling sorry for him again...

I remember Carl in a physics class when our teacher was presenting some information about atoms and electrons. Carl stood up suddenly, awkward and ungainly, but highly excited.

"Ah," he'd said. "Ah! I discern here an apparent universal. The atom is a miniature solar system. If all matter is composed of atoms, then behold! I shall shatter a million tiny worlds full of a zillion tiny beings by biting off just this one fingernail. Behold, catastrophe! I am God." And he fled from the room, talking to himself.

Yeah, he was odd all right.

He graduated just before his fourteenth birthday and instead of giving the usual oration that the valedictorian was supposed to deliver, Carl insisted on playing an original composition he'd written for the piano. It was a real ten-gallon flop, though my mother, who was an accomplished pianist, declared the composition a tremendous achievement.

It lasted far too long for me and most of the audience. Before Carl finished, most of us were looking around at the ceiling, thoroughly bored with the banging chords and Carl's sizzling fingers, prancing up and down the keyboard. What got the audience most, I think, were his fancy head nods and final bow. We sat on our hands solidly and there were even a few boos. We were "Turkey in the Straw" people.

Some months after commencement, Carl came to our door.

"Doctor, sir," he'd said, "Miss Anters, my aunt, has suffered a cardiovascular insult, I surmise, with pains in her thorax and considerable respiratory distress. We would appreciate a professional visit to our domicile."

Dad went down to see her right away. She was having difficulty breathing and she wasn't surprised when dad told her she'd had a heart attack.

"I know," she said, gasping. "My heart is breaking, mainly because of my son, I think, Doctor. Ever since he graduated he's become almost a stranger to me. He hasn't touched the piano. Won't talk to me. He's gone. Walks in the woods, day and night. Says he has to think."

She fell back on the pillow, exhausted. Dad gave her some nitroglycerin for the angina pains and on the way out the door he had a talk with Carl.

"Your mother's very ill," he began, "and she may die. She's spoiled you rotten and waited on you hand and foot all your damned life and now it's going to be your turn to do a little waiting on. YOU chop the wood and YOU go after the mail and YOU go after the groceries. She is not to lift a hand. Understand?"

But Miss Anters died that weekend.

It was several years before we saw Carl again, and again he came to our house.

"Doctor, sir," he begged, "Please, may I have an opportunity to discuss with you an insight which has come to me? I desperately need to present it to someone with some educational and cultural background. Please, sir."

Dad was not one to suffer fools gladly, but he'd just eaten a fine meal with apple pie.

"All right, Carl. Come into the living room and tell us what's on your mind."

I remember some of what Carl had said, but it didn't make much sense then. In essence, he'd claimed to have discovered a brand new art form, one that combined painting and sculpture and music and much more besides. He told us that he'd learned how to build fires so that he could predict exactly every color and contour of the flames from one moment to another.

"I arrange my kindling so it will produce a prelude, shaping the main theme of my composition. I've even learned how to create a counterpoint effect. I've composed three flame symphonies already and I can do them every time - if I have the same kind and right kind of wood. That's the hard part, and also trying to invent a notation that is adequate. I've just got it started, but look here, Doctor."

Carl pulled out a large sheet that looked like a musical score except there were no musical notes on it, just a set of complicated squiggles so far as I could see. He excitedly explained what they meant -

"This one refers to a forked flame, that one to a flame having single apex, this symbol represents the color and duration of the flame, and that's for the sound..."

He also had symbols for tempo. It was far too complicated for me to follow, even though he quit using those big words as he became more excited.

"And these little dots on the score are sparks, Doctor. By using osage orange or sumac wood, I can create a wonderful fanfare of sparks at just the right time. Just think, Doctor, here is the poor man's art form. All he needs is the proper wood and a match and the designs I can give him and a score he can follow from first flicker to ember. I think I've found it. I think I've found my meaning at last. My genius, as I learned at that horrible commencement, is not in music proper, no matter what my aunt told me. I was destined for greater - things to be the inventor and first composer of fire symphonies. Oh, there's much I still have to learn before I can let the world know of my accomplishment. The first new art form in a thousand years!"

27

Carl suddenly stopped talking and looked my father right in the eye. "Am I crazy, Doctor?"

My father was polite, but after he'd ushered Carl out the front door, he made his diagnosis.

"Nutty as a hoot owl," he said.

My mother didn't agree and argued that maybe, just maybe, Carl had stumbled onto something. Dad just smiled.

No one ever found out just how Carl and Elly first became acquainted. Perhaps they met on one of their night walks. I'd like to think that she'd watched from the shadows while he composed, building one little fire after another with different arrangements of sticks, talking to himself and scribbling on a pad, trying to get the notation just right and that one night she had simply walked up and quietly sat down beside him, maybe with a flower offering.

All we really knew was that they were seen together in many odd places and always beside a little fire, never at her house or his, and always after dark. They seemed to have two favorite spots: up on Mount Baldy on any night when there was little wind, and inside the ruins of the old iron furnace smelter in the valley when the wind blew. Long-dead artisans had smelted ingots of pig-iron there using charcoal. It was a spooky kind of place and dirty, but its isolation and draft made it a fine place for Carl to work out his flame symphonies. No one would have seen a fire in those old ruins and it wasn't too far away either, just across the field and behind the saloon.

Some of the kids were curious enough about what was going on to sneak after the pair when they wandered at night, but they reported that nobody was getting any and that there wasn't much going on. Carl just played with the fire or talked and Elly just listened and smiled. Sometimes they held hands, but that was all.

I don't think the grown-ups had any idea that Carl and Elly had been meeting clandestinely at night for several years, until the saloon burned down and ended their idyll.

That was a real humdinger of a fire!

It was almost midnight when the scary cry of "Fire! Fire! Downtown. The Saloon," was passed up the hill, house by house, each man responsible for waking his neighbor.

Men came running down the hill, from everywhere, each carrying a bucket. Others were tearing open the doors of the little tin-sheathed firehouse, pulling the chemical tank cart out and down the street. Men were chopping holes in the side of the saloon. Some were manning a bucket brigade, passing pails hand to hand from the well next door.

There was smoke and flame and hollering. Men began breaking in the front door and carrying out furniture and things like mirrors and chairs, but then they began carrying bottles and whole cases of booze. That wrecked the bucket line immediately as each took whatever he could salvage. There was never such a fire - Never such a long drunk. Half the town was plastered for months.

And of course the building burned up completely. It was almost customary. Our "community center" was a total loss. Sure was exciting!

The next morning the constable took Carl Anters into custody. A hearing was held before the Justice of the Peace upstairs in the Town Hall because there seemed to be some real evidence that the saloon fire had been set. Some charred sticks of kindling smelling of kerosene were found near the smoldering remains of the shed at the back of the saloon and the nightwatch who'd checked the building at 11:30 said he'd met Carl at about that time carrying an armful of cedar sticks. He had asked the young man what he was going to do with the kindling and Carl had said he was going to build a fire.

The Justice of the Peace interrogated Carl just long enough to get him talking about his flame symphonies and then demanded if he had an alibi. Had anyone else been with him at about that time? Carl said yes, that Elly Engstrom and he had created another one of his symphonies in the old iron smelting furnace. He insisted that he certainly hadn't set fire to the saloon.

They brought in the frightened girl and asked her to substantiate the wild story. Elly couldn't say a thing, not even in a whisper. She was completely mute.

The verdict was the same as my father's had been.

In our town it was all right to be nutty so long as you were harmless, but not otherwise. They put handcuffs on Carl and took him away on the next train to Newberry and the insane asylum.

The next morning they took Elly away too. After the hearing, she'd gone slowly home, got a scythe, cut down all her flowers and then started doing the same to all the other gardens in town.

WHITEWATER PETE

In the North Country, no day is so fair as a warm Saturday in late September. The maple hills are mounds of scarlet and gold with just a sprinkling of green from pine.

I remember lying out in the sideyard for an hour on one such Saturday, watching a late bumblebee dusting his bottom on the nasturtiums. He didn't miss a single one and he never buzzed the same one twice. I was picking off some of the orange and maroon flowers, sucking the trumpet stems to see if 'Ol Bumble' had left any honey. I was pleasantly surprised to find that he had when my mother reproached me.

"Son," she said, "Please don't pick those beautiful flowers. They'll all be gone soon enough. I can't see how they possibly escaped that last frost, but let's be grateful."

Mother dreaded the terribly long winters when all the world was black and white and she had to scrape the hoarfrost from the window with her fingernails each morning just to let a ray of sunshine into the house.

She loved all the flowers except wild goldenrod and that she hated with a passion simply because, when it appeared in late August, it meant that our brief summer was coming to a close.

After her protest I knew I'd better leave the premises to do what I'd been postponing for as long as I could. Besides, Mother had a knack for putting an end to would-be mischief by finding some chore for idle hands. Lord, she might even think it was the perfect day for cleaning the chicken coop!

I crawled through the backyard fence and took the back road out past Sliding Rock to visit my friend Pete.

I always thought of Whitewater Pete as "My Friend" - In Capitals - and would often whisper the phrase to myself for reassurance at those boyhood times when I found myself rejected and alone.

Other people in town thought less of him. In their view, "Mr. Pete was just another of the old lumberjack bums left behind when all the pine had been cut and the logging crews moved west to slash hell out of Oregon too."

Mr. Pete had just been too old when it was time to go along.

He was well over seventy when I knew him, tall and thin, but very wiry and he still had that curious spring to his gait that characterizes most of the men who walk in the forest. They were cat-like, ready for anything.

Most people didn't know Whitewater Pete at all. He minded his own business, trapped some, hunted and fished a little, sawed wood and sold it when he could, or built an outhouse, shed or barn for someone who needed help and could pay him a few dollars. He lived in a tight little shack he'd built along the river bank upstream from the village.

Whitewater Pete was very proud. He wouldn't accept charity of any kind and there were times when my dad had to invent work for him so he could make it through another winter without starving. About the only steady income Mr. Pete had was the fifty dollars he got each year for sawing and splitting ten long-cords of maple for the stoves of the Township Hall. And that was a lot of wood for an old man like Mr. Pete.

But Mr. Pete was frugal. Twice a year he went to M.C. Flinn's store and bought a yellow pail of Peerless Tobacco, a pail of lard, a side of bacon, fifteen pounds of dried beans, a lug of dried prunes, some tea and sugar... the necessaries.

Oh yes, and he always bought some hardtack too. I remember that very well because whenever I visited he would break off a small piece of a large black rye wheel, dust it with a pinch of sugar and hand it to me. Hard as a rock, but for an always hungry boy, very very good.

I wondered how Mr. Pete, who had no teeth, could possibly eat it and once I was brave enough to ask him.

"Ho, son," he said, "I just slurp it around in my mouth for a while and then I goom (gum) it. My gooms are so hard now I could bite off a man's ear."

And then he told me a wonderous tale of a fight he'd witnessed between two rivermen, Bad Sam and Bignose Jack, in which each had bitten off one of the other's ears. Mr. Pete sure had some good stories.

I was eight years old when I first met Whitewater Pete.

I was playing lumberjack and riverman in Half-Way Creek, building a logging dam against the flow of one of its springs and floating sticks down into its holding pond.

It had been several decades since the townspeople had seen the last river drive down the Tioga River which flowed through our valley, but most of the old logging dams along the stream could still be seen and I visited them often.

I'd heard the tales of great log jams that formed down at the gorge below our village and how the rivermen stationed every half mile along the banks would give the long "Ai-ee" wail from one to another, summoning help to join in the task of freeing the key log at great risk to their lives. I had even tiptoed along the old log booms that shunted the pine into the sluiceways of the dams.

On Fourths of July, I had seen birling matches where a lumberjack on one end of a log, by rotating it fast and suddenly braking it, would try to dump another jack into the river. I had prowled the remains of tumbled down logging camps, and their old horse barns, hunting for such treasure as a bit of chain or a broken peavy. At the High Banks, I had relived in imagination, the story about how the great piles of timber had cascaded prematurely into the river, carrying ten men to their death. It surely must have been a rough and romantic time.

Anyway, I was completely engrossed in building a dam to recreate the river lore in that tiny rivulet when I was startled by an old man speaking to me.

"No, son," said the voice. "You've got that boom all wrong. Hell, the logs would break through it that way. Look! Slant it down this way..."

And Whitewater Pete got down into the creek and the two of us spent the entire afternoon in fantasy. It was one of the best afternoons in my whole life.

Mr. Pete was an encyclopedia of information about the logging days. One story after another kept spilling from the corner of his mouth where he squeezed the black corn-cob pipe. By the time we had finished building the dam we were both so soaked that Mr. Pete invited me to his shack to dry out before heading for home.

I'll have to admit that the place was kind of ramshackle on the outside, but it was spotless inside.

Hanging on the wall behind the long stove was an axe, a great double bitted one, and a one-man crosscut saw, both gleaming in the shaft of sunlight from the door. Mr. Pete showed me how sharp they were, shaving the hair off his forearm with the axe and letting me feel some of the saw's teeth.

"A good man keeps good tools and he keeps them sharp. Remember that, son!"

Then he showed me some other logging tools: a pike pole, a peavy, used to roll the great logs, and a curious device called a "Comealong" which Mr. Pete claimed, enabled a single man to do the work of five. And Mr. Pete held up his river boots with soles studded with sharp spikes---he called them "corks"---which enabled a man to keep his balance while riding a log down a roaring river.

For me, that little one room shack was thereafter a treasure house and I visited as often as I could.

Mr. Pete and I had another special place where we spent many hours together. It was at the river's edge on a blanket of soft brown needles from a great white pine which towered above us. It was 'OUR PLACE.' Some of his best stories of the old logging days were told there, but we sometimes just sat on a little knoll beneath the great tree, our backs to its bark, in silence and complete contentment. It was nice and quiet.

When I spoke to most people I stuttered pretty badly, but I could talk to that old man with very little trouble.

For one thing he listened.

If I'd ask a question, he'd take out his pipe, blow a smoke ring, cock his head in serious thought and only then offer his considered opinion. He never talked down to me like most big people and he never looked away when I stuttered. We were man to man and Mr. Pete was my friend.

I remember having a hard time talking when trying to ask how come the loggers had left our one big pine there on the knoll when they'd cut all the other ones.

His faded blue eyes never left my face during all my struggle to get the words out and he must have seen my tears for after a long pause he said gruffly, "Every man has his own devil to lick, son. Mine was booze. You got to wrassle 'em down a lot of times before they gives up."

Then he proceeded to answer my question.

He said it was because the big pine leaned too far over the riverbank and, unless you had a good man to fell it, into the drink it'd go. Mr. Pete showed me just how a real sawyer would have angled the "kerf" just right so that the tree, "could be laid out right along the river, pretty as a French girl."

He showed me where you'd make the bottom cut and how deep the notch had to be and how high up the other side the final sawing should be done to, "make the hinge you need." Then he paced off the riverbank to show where the cuts would be made on the fallen trunk.

Squinting up at the great bole of the pine, he said, "And that top log hardly tapers a bit, son. What we used to call a riding log, the kind a man could ride on down the river a mile."

And then Mr. Pete patted the old tree and allowed as he was glad they'd left this last one for us.

But this Saturday afternoon I'd been fooling around watching a bumblebee and sucking nasturtiums, trying to put off going to see Mr. Pete to tell him that they were planning to take him to the county poorhouse.

I had overheard my parents talking about it and when I went to the post office for the mail, Aunt Lizzie was holding forth as usual with her latest gossip.

"Yes," she said, in her nastiest nasal voice. "We've just got to do something about that old bum, Pete. He can't make it through another winter in that disgraceful shack. Doc says he has heart trouble and he hasn't any money and now that we're going to use coal in the Town Hall he won't get his fifty dollars for cutting wood. So how is he going to make it? He'd be better off down there with the other old folks, I say. Won't be so lonesome, I say. He's getting so he won't talk to anybody...anyways to me."

Aunt Lizzie relished the news she was peddling.

"Yes," she continued, "He won't want to go and we may have to get the constable to take him, but the old bum's going to be a town nuisance once the snow comes and, and, and, and,...."

I also remember hearing mother protesting to my father, asking him why the old man couldn't at least have the right to choose, but I was crying too hard in the other room to know how he'd answered.

I had finally decided to go tell Mr. Pete myself so he could light out for some other place. The thought of it emptied me, but I had to tell him.

I'd shaken all the coins from my horsebank for him. I had over six dollars, but it was sure hard to go over the hill to his shack.

The door was open and I saw Mr. Pete, filing his crosscut saw. He took one look at my tear streaked face and made it easy for me.

"I see you've heard the news, eh son?"

I nodded speechlessly and began to sob.

The old man waited until the storm had passed and then said, with a crooked half grin that lifted my spirits, "But I'm not a-goin' to that poorhouse. No Sir, not old Pete. Old Pete's got plans."

He refused my money and we ate some hardtack and drank some tea. I was comforted. Mr. Pete could handle anything.

But when I left his shack he gave me his whittling knife and that bothered me plenty. He told me to take it and carve him something good.

When I got home and talked to my mother about what I'd heard and what Mr. Pete had said, she was most understanding. She told me that my friend did have bad heart trouble, that he probably wouldn't be able to last the winter if he didn't have real care at the county home, that I should know that this was Pete's only hope of sharing another summer with me.

Yes, they were going to take him down to Marquette on Monday, whether he wanted to go or not. I saw her aching for me.

But mother was wrong and Mr. Pete was right. On Monday he was gone when they came after him. Some claim to have heard him giving the old "Ai-ee" call as he rode the log through the rapids past town and into the gorge where they found his body.

All I know for sure was that our great pine had been felled along the river bank and that the riding log was gone... And that Mr. Pete's shack was empty... And so was I.

THE REFORMATION OF BILLY BONES

Most small villages have their town drunk. Ours was Billy Bones. I don't think Bones was his real name, but everyone called him that and it fit.

He was the skinniest man I ever saw, about six feet tall with long gangling broomstick arms. One almost expected to hear him rattle whenever he walked---or staggered.

Everyone in town liked Billy Bones. He was always smiling. Not a silly smile like most drunks have when they're half plastered either, but a big, warm broad-toothed one that lit up his whole face.

Billy Bones was always polite too, always ready to say, "Good morning, my friend," to any man he met or, with a wide sweeping circle, to doff his cap to every woman. Of course, he sometimes fell flat on his face when he did it, but his intentions were honorable.

Then too, there were a few of us who liked him because he'd discovered a way to beat the system, to live without having to work for a living and still be happy.

That wasn't quite true actually, for Billy Bones worked pretty hard, if you could call it work.

He toiled in dandelion time, in rhubarb time or in apple time, gathering the ingredients for the wine he made, gave away, sold and drank. Billy made the best wine you could get, everybody said. It tasted good and had a wallop that would make your ears dance, to say nothing of your belly!

Some claim he fortified it with moonshine he made in a still he had hidden back in Buckeye Woods. If so, no one ever located it and Billy denied its existence.

He made plenty of wine though.

And we kids used to help him, picking dandelions or hauling apples from the wild trees that grew along the edge of the clearing. We did it partly to hear him talk to himself or to hear his town-famous temperance lectures, but mainly because, if we helped him, he'd give us sugar to put on the rhubarb that grew in a big patch behind his house. In the spring, we had a hunger for that rhubarb.

I entered Billy's house only once when my dad had told me to take a bunch of empty gallon jugs to the dump. Billy's rheumy eyes lit up when he saw me hauling my wagon past his house and he begged me to let him have the jugs.

"It'll save me a mite, sonny," he'd said. "I'll just have to get them from the dump anyways."

The inside of his house was something to behold. Two walls were lined with shelves of empty crocks, jugs and bottles.

"I kerlect jugs and bottles," explained Bones with an enormous wink. "It's me hobby."

When I winked back, he took a huge key and opened a six-inch padlock on a half-door hidden back of a curtain behind the stove and told me to take a look into his root cellar. At least another 50 jugs were stashed in there and, judging from the smell, they must have been full. Some kegs and a whiskey barrel were hidden there too.

"Jest a swaller or two to get me through the summer," said Billy. "Sonny, I'm a rich man. Richer than M.C. Flinn, down at the store."

When I hinted that I wouldn't mind having just a taste of all the wealth Billy slammed the door shut fast, sat me down on a big tub and gave me the temperance lecture straight. I'd heard it before, not just from Billy, but from some of my friends who'd memorized parts of it.

"I've got somethin' te put in yer craw, my friend. An' I hopes it sticks like a porkerpine kill (quill). Drink, my friend, is evil…E-vil! The Evilist Evil. Stay away. Don't ya ever take that first swaller or yer a gone goose. One bitty drap an' yer done. Ya know wot likker does in the belly? It eats. It eats yer gizzard. Jest chaws away, chaws away till there's nuthin' north of yer arse but an empty gut. Drink is E-vil! Don't ya take that first swaller."

That was just the beginning. There was more, much more, and by the time he finished he had to drag a jug out from under the bed and drain it.

"Jest a little medicine fer me bowels," he explained.

But he never gave me a drop; never gave any "ta kids er Indians."

It wasn't that Billy was always drunk, but that he was never completely sober. If you went by his cabin about breakfast time, he was usually sitting on the stoop in the morning sunshine, talking to himself.

"Well, Mr. Bones," you could hear him say. "Gonna be 'nother fine day. Yessir. 'Nother fine day. Ya don't look so ver' good and ya don't feel so ver' good, so have yer mornin' coffee, Mr. Bones."

Then he'd pour a tin cupful from a jug, stir it with a bony finger and keep sipping till the smile came back to his face. If it had been a hard night, Billy sometimes needed three or four cups of jug coffee before the world got rosy and the smile returned again. These, with some "booster shots" now and then throughout the day, kept him happy and most of us had to admit that he was the smilingest man in town.

One sight I always treasured was old Billy Bones sitting among the yellow dandelions in the schoolyard each spring, picking them and carefully putting them in a sack as he talked or sang to himself. Sometimes he'd get so happy he'd fling a whole bunch of dandelions into the air and you could hear him laugh as they cascaded down around him.

Another familiar sight was Billy Bones going down the street every afternoon at 4:30 to meet the train. He always hauled a faded red wagon behind him in the summer and a sled in the winter. Everybody knew that under the gunnysack covering the wagon was a jug or bottle that he sold to the trainmen, his regular customers. All of us entered the pretense.

"Going to the store, Billy?" we'd ask.

"Yeah, friend. Got to get me groceries. Got to get me groceries." And then the monstrous wink.

Billy always managed the downhill portion of the journey fairly well, walking stiffly as though following an invisible chalkline. Coming back was another matter entirely. If he'd sold all his dandelion, apple or rhubarb wine, all was well. If not, he went around giving free samples.

"A swaller fer you, me friend, an' a snort fer meself."

On these days Billy and his little red wagon navigated an erratic course back up the hill. We'd see him stop every so often, close one eye and take a bead on wherever he wanted to go next, heading carefully for that spot, always talking to himself. Using familiar teamster's directions, you could hear him steering himself.

"Little more 'Gee' now, Mr. Bones." --- (Go to the right!)

"Now a little more 'Haw' (to the left) and watch out for the tilt, Mr. Bones."

Once when he staggered and sat down, a bystander heard him say, "Danged town anyway, Built their bloody sidewalks too close to me ass, they did. Goin' sue 'em! That's wot Mr. Bones'll do. Sue 'em!"

Somehow he always made it back to his house. Year-after-year that daily journey was part of the rhythm of our days.

So long as Billy stuck to his wine he had the system beat, but as years wore by, the trip back up the hill became more and more arduous. To fortify himself for the ordeal, the old man began stopping off at Higley's Saloon, buying a drink from the day's proceeds and cadging several more from the other boozers hanging out there.

They'd say, "Billy, give us yer temperance lecture and we'll buy you a drink" or "Billy, tell us about the time the bear got you up a tree."

That bear story was a dandy because Billy always acted it out as he told it. How he was a-walkin' down by Hek's spring when this she-bear took after him and how he jumped up and grabbed that branch and swung himself up and how the she-bear began a-drinkin' the liquor from the jug he'd dropped and...They say that nobody could put on a drunken bear act so "natural

The more polluted Billy became the better he preached and acted. He got plenty of free drinks too. Some were even on the house.

They say that once when he was telling the bear story and showing how he'd jumped for the limb, Billy had grabbed the wagon-wheel chandelier and pulled it crashing down from the ceiling in a shower of plaster. Didn't faze him a bit. Billy didn't even pause.

"Rotten branch," he said, and went on with the story.

The heavier drinking unfortunately took its inevitable toll. The smile left Billy's face and he began to stagger worse. He mumbled rather than spoke. Somedays he missed his daily journey down the street. Some nights he never got home at all or the night-watch would find him sprawled in the snow halfway up the hill.

Always skin and bones, he was now just bones, a sodden scarecrow. The whole town felt bad about what was happening and my dad went down to the saloon and told the proprietor not to give Billy another drink or he'd see that he wouldn't get his license next time around.

"Hell, Doc, I'm not giving him nothing," protested the saloon keeper. "Billy's been drinking moonshine and Lydia Pinkham's Vegetable Compound mostly. Them'll kill anybody, take it enough."

We all figured he'd be a gonner before spring.

Then one evening toward the end of winter, I was over with my father in his dispensary admiring Mrs. Saavonen's tapeworm, which he had described at suppertime in spite of my mother's protests. (Dad really liked to share some of the more gory details of his medical practice at mealtimes.)

He was telling me about it.

"These Finns from the Old Country like raw fish and even when they boil them they don't cook 'em long enough, no matter what I try to tell them. Well, Mrs. Saavonen's been doing poorly for some months now, getting thinner and thinner at the same time she's eating more and more, so I suspected what was wrong with her. Gave her a hell of a purge - a concoction of castor oil, calomel and a squirt of croton oil. Sure enough, fifteen minutes later there was the end of that tapeworm in her stool with more hanging out her tail. Well, I wanted to get the head so I just kept tugging at it, hauling it hand over hand like you pull in a pike on a line. Must be six, seven yards of it in that jar."

It looked to me like a long, tangled yellow-white noodle and I was about to ask if he'd got the head out too when someone screamed in the hallway and in came Billy Bones, flinging himself at dad's feet.

"Got to help me, Doc! Got to help ol' Billy. Got the snakes awful bad. Watch out, Doc! There's a red one a comin' over yer shoulder!" He screamed again.

Billy's eyes were as white as a scared horse's. He was shaking all over, jerking in stark terror.

I'd never seen delirium tremens before and I hoped that I'd never see anything like them again. Dad gentled the old man and gave him a shot of morphine. We hitched up the horse and took Billy to the jail in the Town Hall where the constable could keep an eye on him until he sobered up. The constable helped dad lay Billy on a cot. He was out cold.

Dad was quiet all the way back from the jail, but he kept biting his lip the way he always did when he was mad about something or when he was really determined.

Things began happening pretty fast next day.

Legal or not, dad got some men to clean out every jug and bottle from old Billy's house. They hauled them to the dump and smashed them, but we later learned that they hadn't found the half-door to the root cellar behind the curtain.

Dad got Mrs. Jensen who took in boarders, including our preacher, to agree to give Billy a try-out.

"We'll sober him up and clean him up, but you and the preacher have got to 'feed him up' and keep him that way," dad said, paying her generously.

Then he marched over to Flinn's Store to try and persuade Mr. Flinn to give Billy a job as a delivery boy. It was a hard sell situation.

"You're crazy, Doctor," said Mr. Flinn when dad proposed the idea.

"That drunken old bum couldn't take an order, let alone deliver it somewhere."

"I promise you that he'll be clean and sober," said dad. "Let him go along with your regular driver at first. We'll get him dried out and I'll pay his salary."

That offer did the trick and Billy had a chance for a job and a fresh start.

Dad went to the ladies who ran the Methodist Ladies Aid and the Catholic Order of the Eastern Star to get them to organize what came to be called the "Billy Watch." If any of their membership saw Billy Bones with his little red wagon or his sled, going after his "groceries" or staggering, or heading for the saloon or hanging around the depot, they were to round him up and take him back to the boarding house immediately. If he gave any of them any trouble, they were to get the constable to take him. Billy wasn't to go any further down the street than the schoolyard and certainly nowhere near the saloon or the depot. Dad was emphatic and hinted strongly that if any of them ever wanted his medical services in the future they had better cooperate.

Dad finally called on the preacher and the priest.

"Damned if I know what religion Billy belongs to, if any, but somehow I want you to get him started going to church even if you have to kidnap him to get him there. Get him on the wagon and save his bloody soul!"

They both laughed and promised to do whatever they could.

This done, Dad marched on over to the jail and proceeded to give Billy "blue-shirted hell."

He told him, in no uncertain terms, that he'd never save him from the snakes again, that he'd never get out of jail unless he swore never to take another drink. And there was a lot more. He told Billy what he'd done with his jugs and about the new life he'd arranged for him and then he left him in jail "just to think about it" for a week before going to see him again.

The whole town was agog and they did a lot of talking during that week Billy was in jail. Most were pretty pessimistic. So was dad, privately of course.

"Oh, I don't really have much hope," he said "but that poor old fellow ought to have one chance anyway. Maybe the town can pull it off. We'll see."

And we saw. There were miracles still in the land and the reformation of Billy Bones was one of them. Oh, there were some pretty shaky moments at first and a few times when the "Billy Watch" had to go into action, but it soon became apparent that Billy was really changing his ways and becoming a new man.

For one thing he was eating right, probably for the first time in his life, and his job brought him into all the better homes of the community where he found great interest and approval and encouragement for the change that was occurring. Everyone asked him how he was doing and they all smelled his breath to make sure.

"Not a swaller," he'd tell them proudly. "Haint had a swaller o' likker since I quit. Old Billy Bones knows better now. Not goin' take that first drop neither, no sirree."

Billy had become sort of a civic project.

Basking in the glow of our acceptance and interest, Billy bloomed. Pink returned to his cheeks, fading the purple from his nose. M.C. Flinn fired the other driver and let Billy take the orders and make the deliveries all by himself - at smaller wages than he'd paid before of course. Flinn's only complaint was that Billy took longer enroute than he should have. Everybody knew why though. Billy couldn't just take an order and leave. He had to pass the time of day, had to do a little preaching on the e-vils of drink and he had revised and improved his old sermon by personalizing it.

"Yep, friend, jus' look at old Billy Bones here now an' 'member how he wuz - Jus' a old bum, stinkoed up day 'n night, a lyin' in the snow so snockered couldn't even git up, a-fearin' them snakes an' goin' ta jail. The e-vils of drink, my friend. Don't you never take that first swaller."

He often let one of us kids make his rounds with him and he'd lecture us all over town.

Billy also got religion real bad. After visiting both the Catholic and Methodist-Episcopal churches, he chose the latter.

Perhaps he was influenced by his fellow boarder, the preacher, but mainly, according to Billy, "Because them Mefordists holler louder and lay it on me stronger-like."

Billy never missed a church service or a Men's Bible Class. He liked going. Liked being dressed up. After a couple of months he even joined the church and got baptized, an experience that affected him greatly.

"Been washed in the blood of the lamb, friend," he'd tell anyone who'd listen. "Washed clean as the driven snow, friend. Ol' Billy's bin saved."

One Sunday, Billy came to church in a brand new blue-serge suit, clean as a whistle from a long Finnish sauna the night before, and very solemn. He was to take his first communion.

When the old organ began to shake the church and the choir sang,
"Break Thou the bread of life
"Dear Lord for me
"As Thou didst break the loaves
"beside the sea,"
the tears began rolling down Billy's pink cheeks as he and several others

walked slowly up front and kneeled on the step below the altar to receive the sacrament. He wept even more when the preacher intoned the ancient words of comfort:

"Ye that do truly and earnestly repent of your sins, and are in love and charity with your neighbors, and intend to lead a new life..."

The service droned on until the preacher broke the bread and put it to Billy's lips and gave him the cup of wine, saying, "Drink this in remembrance that Christ's blood was shed for thee, and be thankful."

Billy hesitated for only an instant.

He didn't go back to the boarding house after church and he didn't show up for work at the store next morning. Billy Bones simply disappeared. No one ever saw hide nor hair nor bone of him again.

Oh, someone said that someone had told them that someone had seen an old bum lugging a packsack and a jug up the railroad tracks way over by Nestoria, but whether it was Billy Bones or not we never knew. The great forest that hugged our village had swallowed up more than one of those who had wandered in it drunkenly. Most of the people in town figured that was what had happened to poor old Bones. It was too bad.

The truth often provides a miserable ending for our personal tales even when they seem to be ending happily and this was probably the case with Billy Bones. So I deliberately made up another ending for the story because I didn't like the probable ending. I've told it over and over and over again until even I believe it. It goes like this:

Billy didn't go back to the boarding house after church and he didn't show up for work the next morning either. Instead they found him in his old place in the schoolyard, sitting in a patch of yellow dandelions with an empty jug beside him.

"Yep, friend," he said, flinging a dandelion over his shoulder happily, "Like I allus say, don't you ever take thet first swaller. For drink, it is E-vil!"

BATS

Long before I read "Dracula" or explored some of the caverns of Kentucky, I was fascinated by bats.

Every summer evening about dusk the air would be full of them, swooping and soaring in blurred circles as they fed on mosquitos that infested the little town where I lived as a boy.

My friends and I tried to catch them by flinging our caps high in the air. Only one did I actually catch, doubtless a deaf one, for their sonar is incredibly efficient. We kept it out in the barn for a week in a screened box, hidden secretly, for my mother and grandmother were deathly afraid of the "critters." My father didn't like them either. He said they had rabies.

The bat I had was a quaint little creature, covered with fur, (and a few lice), except for black leather wings. His face was like that of a tiny human and when I held him, I could feel his heart throbbing so fast it seemed to buzz. He wouldn't eat the houseflies or mosquitoes we caught. He evidently had to catch them on the wing, so he died. For two minutes I grieved deeply for my little friend, Oscar.

As I mentioned, my grandmother Gage was petrified by bats. She loved to sit out on the front porch in the evening and watch the children, the buggies going by or Old Billy Bones staggering home from the tavern. She'd cluck her tongue at him, call us to her side and give us her temperance lecture.

"See that man, children?" she'd say. "He'll come to a bad end. That likker is eating holes all over his insides right now. Mark my words, now, someday he'll spring a leak and all his giblets will come oozing out of the holes."

We used to follow Old Billy, hoping to witness the puncture, but it never happened. He just disappeared on his way home from church one Sunday.

When the bats started flying near the end of July, grandma Gage no longer dared sit on the porch. Neither did my mother. They were afraid the bats would get in their hair. "Bats always go for a woman's hair," Grandma said, "They lay eggs in it."

Once she tried wearing the long hood with the isinglass peepholes that we used when the temperature went down to 30 and 40 degrees below zero.

The hood was just too hot and she had to be content with peering out the bay window. This made her so irritable that we had to be very careful whenever we got near her.

Grandma was the sweetest old lady in lavender and lace that ever graced a rocking chair, but she had one little eccentricity. She liked to stick needles in the hind ends of anyone who came within striking distance when she was sewing. Then she'd chuckle to herself for hours. I should tell you about the time the preacher....but back to the bats.

Occasionally, really very rarely, a bat would get into the house. Then pandemonium! My father would get the broom and start swinging, getting madder with each miss. The women would scream and throw something over their hair - anything. I remember seeing my Grandma's legs for the first time when she pulled up her long skirts and ran from the room, looking upside down. Another time she tried to burrow under the rug, and I remember hoping the bat would try to go up her pantaloons. It was always very exciting.

Finally my father, exhausted from his efforts, would yell at them to shut-up, insisting that bats didn't get into women's hair, that it was all nonsense, that he'd wait until daylight and then he'd pick the damn thing off the ceiling or wherever the bastard went to roost. More screams and tears and profanity.

Very, Very exciting - almost as good as the Fourth of July. I remember leaving the woodshed door open some evenings in the hope that a bat would enter.

The morning after one of these encounters, while the women still lay abed with the sheets over their heads, it was our job to make a complete search of the house. Supervised by father, and with a dime reward to the kid who first spotted the little beast, we usually managed to locate the bat. We never did find it hanging from the ceiling. It never made any sense to me that it might. There was no toehold. It was usually hanging upside down from the upper corner of a door frame or one of the windows.

Father would kill it, the women would get up, and finally we had breakfast. There was just one time when the bat completely disappeared. We searched and re-searched that house, basement to attic, but no bat. There were no open windows through which it might have escaped. No one had opened the door. IT was in the house! A long hunt and a longer night followed. We looked again for it next morning.

Everywhere.

No bat.

Finally my father went to the bedroom, threw the covers off my trembling mother, commanded her to get the hell downstairs and make him some breakfast. He should have been at work two hours before. She wept and shook all through the meal. My father felt some remorse at his roughness, but he was "full fed" by this time.

"Now look, dear," he said with an enormous patient sigh, "Let's be reasonable. That bat will not get in your hair. Bats don't get in people's hair. They sleep all day. They will not move all day. I'll try to find it again after I get home at noon. Let me say it again - BATS DON'T GET INTO PEOPLE'S HAIR." He left the house.

When my mother finally stopped sobbing and shaking, she went to my grandmother's room while I eavesdropped in the hall. I heard my father's argument all over again as mother tried to persuade Grandma to come out from under the covers. "Bats don't really get in people's hair. They sleep all day. He'll kill it when he gets home. Bats don't get in people's hair." Well, Grandma did get up eventually and had her breakfast, though she wore a kerchief. I went out to play for a bit and when I returned, my mother and grandmother were getting dressed to leave.

"We'll be back in an hour or so," my mother said. "We have to go see Mrs. Duggan, poor thing. She's ailing and I'm fetching her some broth."

"Yes," said Grandma, "and we're getting out of this bug bat-house."

She went into the hall, put on her hat and let forth with the scream of screams.

The bat was in her hat.

MRS. MURPHY GETS A BATH

It was after 4:00 p.m. when my father stumped heavily into the house and dropped his two black bags; the pill case and the instrument satchel, on the floor.

He wrestled out of his heavy beaverskin coat and hung it with the black fur hat on the hall tree.

"Cully," he said to me, "I'm bushed. You'll have to unharness Billy from the buckboard and feed and water him. Give him an extra scoop of oats. He's had a rough day too. He's out front."

I was glad to do it because it gave me a chance to drive around to the barnyard. I never usually handled the reins unless dad was with me. I was only twelve. That afternoon the old horse was so tired that I had no trouble with him at all except when I went to back the buckboard into the carriage shed. Billy wanted to go to the stable right away, buckboard and all, but I finally managed to get him unharnessed.

I unhooked the tugs and led Billy into the big box stall, but not until I'd removed the bit from his mouth and put on the halter. It's tough trying to put a halter on a horse when he's eating oats, but you can take off the harness and horsecollar all right. I had to jump though to put these up on their hooks, high on the wall. I climbed up into the hayloft and pitched down an extra big pile of hay through the hole in the ceiling of the box stall. I had to pump and carry five pails of water before Billy was satisfied and ready to let me rub him down.

When I returned to the house, dad was in his Morris chair with his feet up on the hassock, talking to my mother. He was making entries in a little black notebook.

"Did pretty well today, Edith. Took in $23. Of course, fifteen was from Einer Pesonen for that breach baby case two years ago. He was out by the road at Halfway Creek and had the money in his hand. Said he'd just got paid for a carload of pulp."

My father never sent out a bill in his life, but he recorded all the money that was owed him in the pages of that little black notebook and he knew who hadn't paid.

I remember that he'd once pointed to a grown man walking up the sidewalk in front of our house.

"See that bugger? He's not paid for yet!"

But he never dunned any of his patients. He served a territory as large as Rhode Island, most of it wilderness, and it seemed to us that he was always tired.

Dad certainly was that day for he'd been out half the night on a baby case. He'd just leaned back in his chair when there was a knock at the front door.

"Another damned wart," he growled. "Why don't they come at office hours? If it's old lady Pascoe with her usual Monday afternoon headache, I'll give her short shrift!"

But dad's face lit up when he opened the door. It was Father Hassel, the Catholic priest, hoping for his weekly chess game, a stout glass of whiskey, a good cigar and some good conversation. In the barren wilds that both of them served, educated people could be counted on one hand. The need to share insights above the bread and butter level was almost a craving.

So whenever they could manage it, my father and the priest got together. Sometimes dad would go down to see Father Hassel, but more often the priest came to our house, hopefully he teased, to convert my father away from his avowed agnosticism, but mainly to escape his parish duties and his housekeeper for the procession of priests who served our village. Not that Father Hassel was very vulnerable... He was about sixty, red cheeked, white haired and did his utmost to serve his people.

It was said that he didn't holler much about purgatory or pass out tough penances or ask for more money than the French Canadians and Indians who came to Mass or confession could spare.

Dad and Father Hassel had met often at the bedsides of dying patients, had ridden cabooses to far away junctions and they had genuine respect and affection for each other.

One of the house rules was that when Father Hassel came to visit we had to clear out to the kitchen so they would be undisturbed in their chess game and so they could speak freely. I used to like to hear them talk though, and would often sneak up the back stairs and tiptoe down the front ones to sit on my dad's bed behind the curtains where I could listen. On this particular occasion they were talking about old Bridget Murphy who lived uptown in one of the mining company's old houses.

"Father," said my dad, "You've got to do something about Mrs. Murphy. Yesterday her neighbors heard her cow bellowing, probably because it hadn't been milked for some time, and after they looked in on her they called me. She was moaning and a bit bloated when I went in. Bowels hadn't moved for almost a week, she said, and she was sure she's going to die. I gave her castor oil and calomel and she'll probably be all right in a day or two, but you'd better go see her."

The priest nodded.

"I'll go up after supper," he said, "even though she hears only one Mass a year at most and comes to confession only when there's an eclipse or something. Which is all right with me, Doctor. The only sins she ever confesses are thirty years old and she uses my time to revel in her old memories of fornication. But I'll go see her."

I grinned, hiding there behind the curtains. I knew what that meant.

Old Bridget Murphy was a true character in a village filled with them. She was loud and profane and we boys used to like to go sit on her porch on a summer afternoon to hear her tell of the glorious "loving" she used to get from her late husband, "Misther Michael Murphy, God rist his black sowl."

The old woman would sit there in her rocker, always wearing a pair of faded scarlet shoes, rocking away and chuckling evilly as she told her tales. It was educational.

"Ah, me late husband, Misther Michael Murphy, he was a man," she'd say. "That he was, that he was. A harrd worker, he was, and a fighter to be sure and when the whiskey was in him, a mean divil, but ah me bhoys, he was a booger in bed. He'd grab me, he would, and nail me a yellin' to the floor. That he would. Sivin times in a row once. Sivin, I tell you and I felt ivery last one a shakin' me teeth. Did I ever tell you bhoys 'bout the time....?"

Of course she had, but she told us again and again anyway. Mister Murphy must have indeed been quite a man.

Bridget Murphy also liked to sing and she taught us some noble bawdy ballads... And woe to the youth who took his girl past her house when old Bridget was on the porch. Keeping time to their steps, the lewd old woman would chant in a voice you could hear a quarter mile away, "Take down yer pants, Colleen, and give the bhoy a chance. Take down yer pants and give the bhoy a chance."

How embarrassing!

Sometimes, on St. Patrick's Day she'd paint a bright green stripe around the back of Paddy, her pet pig. Sometimes she painted its hind end a bright orange. Bridget liked color. She always had a red geranium in her window, summer or winter.

My father continued, "Well, now," he said. "I'm not concerned with the old girl's bloody soul or sins, or even her health, for all that matter, but in all my life, Father, and I've been in some pretty terrible homes, I've never seen such a dirty place or such a dirty old woman. Why, I could hardly bear to lift her nightgown to palpate her abdomen. Father, she's a crust on her so thick it almost shines. And the stench! I've got a strong nose, Father, but I could hardly wait to get out of there. I'll bet she hasn't bathed for years. You've got to give her a bath, I tell you. And clear out and clean out that whole place. That damn pig of hers was in and out of the room constantly and, God help me, so were the chickens. I had to shoo away one old hen that was roosting on the headboard. It's terrible.

The priest moved his Queen's knight to the Bishop's fourth and puffed his cigar thoughtfully.

"The Irish do not have the same feeling about dirt as we do, Doctor. I know she smells pretty high. Had to aerate the confessional last time she came. But surely this is your province as the health officer and not mine."

Dad moved a pawn up to challenge the knight.

"Do you want me to sic Aunt Lizzie and the Methodist Ladies Aid on poor old Bridget and shame all the good Catholics in this town who ought to be taking care of their own?" dad asked. "Aunt Lizzie would love the job and so would all the other Protestant women."

"You're right, Doctor.

"Check!

"I'll talk to Mrs. LaFon and see if the Sisters of St. Mary won't tackle it. But if I know Bridget, we may have to call you to anesthetize her so we can get her in the tub - if she has a tub, which I doubt. And besides, she's sick, isn't she, Doctor? Could she stand the shock of such a bath? And if she could, what about the pig and those chickens? If I know old Bridget, she'll go right back to her old ways.

"Check again."

"Tell you what we'll do," my father said, moving his King out of danger. "I'll tell Bridget that she's very sick and in danger of dying and that she has to go to the hospital in Ishpeming immediately. They'll give her the bath of her life there and you can even administer the last rites before she goes if you want to. Bridget's really not that sick, as I said, but that'll get her out of the house so I can get some men to fix up the barn and pig and chicken house. Bridget says the only reason she lets the pig and biddies into the house is because the outbuildings are so cold and drafty now with winter coming on so fast.

You get your women to clean that house from top to bottom and I'll take care of the rest. Have you ever been in her house, Father?"

The priest shook his head.

"Well," said my father, "all the buildings are inter-connected. Mike Murphy bought that company house when the mine shut down, added a woodshed to it, added a log barn to the shed and there's where Bridget keeps her cow, added a pig house to the barn, and ended the string with a chicken house. They're all connected, though there are doors for each part. Seemed like a good idea in this land of forty below winters. Anyway, that's why the pigs and chickens come into the house proper. I wonder that the cow hasn't!"

The next few days were busy ones with dad supervising the men repairing the outbuildings and Father Hassel overseeing the Sisters of St. Mary as they cleaned the house. Dad grinned when he got the phone call from the hospital.

"Well, Bridget's had her bath," he told my mother. "The nurses down there say they won't ever forgive me. They found a slight impaction in the bowel, but nothing serious and the old gal's all right now and yelling to come home. By tomorrow everything should be spic and span. The barn, pig shed and chicken coops are all as tight as a drum. What a job! Good thing it's only the first week in November. Bridget and her brood should be snug all winter."

Two days after Mrs. Murphy returned home, Father Hassel knocked on the door early in the morning.

"Doctor," he said, "I'm afraid our good deed has had an evil ending. The shock of that bath and the clean house were probably too much for Bridget to take. Her neighbors say there's no smoke coming from her chimney and the door is locked and nobody answers their calls. Will you come up with me, please?"

When my dad returned, mother ran to the door.

"Is it true? Is the old lady dead?"

Dad shook his head ruefully then roared with laughter.

"No, Bridget's fine. She told us she'd got to feeling too lonesome for her pig, Paddy, and all her biddies. We found her wrapped in blankets out in the barn with her cow and pig and chickens all around her, and she was happily smoking an old corncob pipe. Said she couldn't bear to dirty up that nice clean house... Hell, you can't ever get the best of the Irish!"

U. P. BAKKABALL

There was very little to do in our small forest village during "the long white," those nine months when snow and ice covered everything. Hunting and fishing stopped when the deep cold set in and great drifts smothered the land. But we did have bakkaball (basketball). The Finn kids never seemed to be able to handle the pronunciation of the 'sk' sound although they could put it together pretty well in one of their favorite epithets "buskan hosu" (shit pants).

Anyway, football and baseball were strictly summertime things diddled at by little kids, but of very little importance. Bakkaball was our serious sport.

All of us played bakkaball. We played in the snow until it was packed down solid. It never did get hard enough to dribble on, not that we ever had a ball that anyone could dribble with anyway. We 'created' our own balls, rolled-up burlap bags tied with a string, a ball of rags some mother had planned to use for weaving a carpet... In a pinch we used ten-inch snowballs, packed tight, but these weren't very permanent and when you caught a teammate's pass it usually knocked you on your tail. Once we used a blown up pig's bladder, but it was too light to go through the potato-basket hoop nailed to the barn door.

Our games rarely had more than four players and more often only two. It was one-on-one and devil take the hindmost. No referee! No fouls! We took turns throwing the ball up in the air and then fought like wildcats in the snow until somehow the "ball" went through the hoop. Then we threw it aloft again and fought some more.

Slug, bang, slash; get the ball anyway you could. Body contact? Of course! Knock him down and wrestle the ball away. There was only one thing you couldn't do: no fair kicking in the crotch!

We played bakkaball even when it was thirty below. We sometimes even got up a sweat running around in our heavy clothing and swampers. As I remember, there wasn't a lot of team play even when we chose up sides. Oh, you might occasionally pass the ball to a teammate if you knew some opposing player was about to knock you down, but otherwise you tucked it under your arm and charged over your opponents until you got close enough to the barn door to have a chance to shoot. Without referees there was no one to toss the ball in the air after a basket was made so the opposing jumpers held the ball jointly as the rest counted - one, two, three and then they were supposed to toss it straight up. No one ever did and we had more good fights as a result of those jump balls than at any other part of the game.

It was mayhem in the snow. Finn kids, Indian kids, French Canadin frogs; we all played bakkaball throughout the winter.

The only ones who played bakkaball indoors were members of our town team. Each of the villages had a team of big men in their twenties or early thirties - lumber-jacks, miners, farmers - all with monstrous muscles. They had no gym suits, but played instead in their long winter underwear, red or dirty white, in the large meeting room of our Town Hall. How they could bear to practice once a week and play once a week after their terribly strenuous labors each day was beyond my com-prehension. Perhaps bakkaball provided the only opportunity to fight like hell, legally. All of us kids used to sneak down to the Town Hall to watch them practice and, if we could manage an extra ten cents which was seldom, we'd go to see them play some team from another town.

Play?

It was slaughter!

At these team games there was always a referee, a very brave, or very stupid, or sometimes just half-drunk fellow. No man in his right mind would want to take such an assignment. I remember one referee throwing up his hands and quitting on the spot after getting knocked down twice, first by a member of one team and then by someone from the other. The referee had failed to recognize the limits of his authori-ty and made a mistake by calling a couple of fouls. Referees were there to throw jump balls, not to call fouls. After they'd heaved him out an open window into the snow the game continued with a new referee shanghaied from the crowd of onlookers. They had six referees that night.

Many of the games were never completed, but ended in a gang fight always won, if that's the word to use, by the home team and their loyal fans who had broken through the chicken wire barrier that separated the stage from the playing floor.

The hall had a low ceiling too, so no one ever arched a shot. The players aimed directly at the basket, expecting to miss it, but hoping that someone could put the ball through from the melee beneath the hoop. They took that first shot from the far end of the floor, shooting the ball from between their legs, then rushing in to clobber the nearest opponent.

Hazardous to the health too was the big pot-bellied stove at one side of the play-ing floor. The men made a wide dribble around the red glow of its cast iron hulk if they could and there were four men stationed nearby who were supposed to heave back any player who might be flung against it. The guards often failed in their duty when it seemed pretty certain to be their asses that got burned. They'd flinch or step aside at the last moment and you'd hear the agonized howl of a roasted half-breed Indian or a broiled Finn.

And another brawl would always begin whenever that happened...

Our town constable, Charley Olafson, was six feet tall and three feet wide and he came complete with silver star on his massive chest. Charley usually did his best to maintain some semblance of order or at least prevent murder at those games and most of the time he succeeded to some degree.

A very strong man, Charley would pick up a combatant in each hand, lift them from the floor and bang their heads together. He always felt bad when he had to do it twice. He prided himself on being able to get it right the first time. Charley was a man of peace. He just wanted to render people helpless, not unconscious. He wasn't always able to do so, though. When eight or ten men were slugging it out with each other at the same time, Charley regretted only having two hands.

I remember one real bad riot vividly. The other town team had come with a sizeable contingent of burly supporters and they hogged all the best seats on the stage behind the chicken wire next to the basket. Our team was ahead by just a few points when one of their fans began aiming his miner's carbide lantern, one with a big bull's-eye lens, right into the eyes of our players every time they were ready to shoot. All hell broke loose. The chicken wire was ripped down and the whole place became a madhouse of fighting men with me and the other kids cowering bug-eyed in a corner.

Out came Charley, this time with gun in hand, and he fired a shot through the open window to get their attention.

"What's the trouble, boys? What's the trouble?"

Our team went over to answer his question. They took away his gun, pitched it and Charley out through the open window and returned to the fray. I don't know who won because I ran home.

That's how they played bakkaball in the U.P. when I was a boy!

CIVILIZATION COMES TO OUR TOWN

Culture, 'with a capital C,' came to our forest village in the lissome form of Miss Lorelie Young, the new English teacher. Miss Lorry was from Boston and fresh out of Bryn Mawr or some other eastern finishing school.

How she happened to end up in our town I never found out, but I know that she, an incurable romantic, was hunting for adventure out west among the cowboys and Indians and such.

We had Indians and half-breeds, all right, but the closest thing to a cowboy she ever saw was me riding Billy back from duck hunting on Splatterdock Lake with my shotgun slung over my shoulder. Miss Lorry didn't seem to mind that ours was not the Wild West of her dreams. It was wild enough with bears coming into town to raid the apple trees and the wolves chasing deer on the hills behind the schoolhouse, shattering the night air with their howls. To her, everything was primitively fascinating, completely different than anything she had ever known.

Miss Lorry said she had travelled extensively in Europe and even to Egypt, but that she'd never seen anything like this. Intensely curious about how we lived and completely unafraid, she immersed herself in our activities.

All us high school kids, boys and girls alike, fell in love with Miss Lorry almost immediately. A strange white being from outer space had come to our town and wanted to know how we lived. We told her and showed her and she in turn told us of life in the big city and foreign lands... Not that there wasn't some testing.

The Finn girls parboiled her in a sauna, made her whip herself afterwards with cedar branches and jump naked into the pond. They showed her how to churn butter and grinned when her arms almost broke from pushing the plunger up and down. The Indian girls taught her how to make a moccasin out of deer hide by chewing the leather until it was soft and supple. The French Canadian girls taught her bawdy French songs and took her to Mass and into their homes to eat crusts smeared with bacon grease instead of butter. She even learned how to milk a cow.

The high school boys gave her a few rough times before surrendering to her charm and enthusiasm. I remember a nature hike she sponsored after school to gather material for an English theme. About 15 of us boys and girls, but mostly boys, took her past Sliding Rock, had her climb the rock face of Mount Baldy along the ledges, jump ditches, hop on clumps of saw grass across a swamp and go through the tangle of a cedar swamp to get to Fish Lake.

Scratched and soiled, Miss Lorry loved every bit of the ordeal and squealed like the other girls when we boys stripped and took a swim.

On the way back along a well trodden path, she asked about everything; the names of the trees and shrubs and flowers, how you snared rabbits, the habits of grouse.

Was it true, she asked, that you could boil water in a birch bark basket without having the bark catch fire?

We showed her that it was - that the heat went into the water and wouldn't char the bark. We had her taste the pulp of a Jack in the Pulpit, setting her mouth on fire, and then we showed her that when boiled in that birch bark basket it was sweet as a potato. Once she picked up a rabbit dropping, well dried, and asked if that nut were good to eat. Of course we assured her that it was. She nibbled it delicately, saying that it was a little bitter and offering the rest of it to Okarri who gallantly chewed it down - much to our admiration and amusement.

About half way back to town, we jumped a deer that bounded gracefully away, a sight which triggered all the boys into aiming imaginary guns at it. Miss Lorry was appalled.

"How can you kill such a beautiful creature!" she exclaimed.

We thought she was asking for information...

"Why," said one of us, "You aim for a spot just behind the front shoulder, or the neck if you're close enough. Or, if you got a miner's carbide light, you can shine 'em at night and shoot them between the eyes. Old Man Kalla has built himself a perch up in an elm tree by the lake clearing and he shoots them in the back when they come out a dusk to feed. Or, if you can steal some telephone or telegraph wire, you can make a big noose out of it and put it across a runway fastened to a strong maple sapling."

"Yah," said another boy, Pierre Rameau I think, "mon granpere, he told me that when he was a young man, he used to make pits in their runways and have some sharp stakes that the deer would fall on and kill themselves. My granpere, he said he never had money for shell and you got to eat."

All of us nodded, boys and girls alike. Without deer meat how could you make it through the winter?

Miss Lorry tried to understand and jotted down a few sentences in the little notebook she always carried. She said she might write a book about us someday.

She certainly kept gathering material for such a book. She learned some words and phrases of Finnish and found ways of getting into some Finn homes for coffee and korpua or fish-eye soup or their delectable soft cheese and smoked fish. After word got around that she wasn't "stuck up" and knew all the ancient Finnish epic of the Kalevala and had even visited Helsinki, doors were opened to her that had never been opened to any but another Finn. She went several times to the Finnish Lutheran church and talked at length with the preacher who said afterwards that she was a good woman. Miss Lorry even attended a Holy Roller (Holy Jumper), service once in their little white church, amazed and delighted by the religious frenzy of those who writhed on the floor, regretting their evil ways, or those climbing the pillars of the church porch, yelling to God to let them into heaven. She even tried to sing the strange hymns and put a whole dollar in the collection plate.

Miss Lorry loved our autumn days with the scarlet maple and yellow birch leaves against a background of green pine and firs. Every Saturday she walked in the forest and by the blue lakes, usually with three or four of us tagging along. I remember once that we took our lunch along over to Horseshoe Lake and stopped in to see old Arne Nevola who had a cabin there.

Arne was pretty close to being a hermit.

He was a short man with faded brown eyes, half hidden by a tangle of hair and beard. We were fixing to share our sandwiches with him, but he refused. He'd just caught a handful of trout, he said, and was about to cook them. He offered us coffee. Miss Lorry looked aghast as old Arne put a chunk of salt pork into the pan on the stove, waited till it sizzled, then took each trout, squeezed it hard (they were uncleaned), and dropped it into the pan. He said something in Finnish and we translated for Miss Lorry.

"Arne says you gotta always squeeze 'em till they squeak before you cook 'em."

The old man ate the trout like we eat sweet corn. No fork. Arne didn't believe in forks.

"Forks leak," he told us.

Miss Lorry took notes.

Miss Lorry was an excellent though highly unorthodox teacher. Appalled by the dog-eared texts in English and American Literature that were provided by the school board, she sent home for huge boxes of her own books and placed them in the assembly room for all to read. One of them was "Bartlett's Quotations," which got more use than any other since no one could come to class unless they came with a quotation they had memorized. We prowled through that book over and over again, looking for one that would please her or that would make the class laugh. I collected one of the latter from Shakespeare: "Phew, methinks I smell of horsepiss!" The class roared. Miss Lorry never batted an eye.

She soon discovered that most of the kids had never willingly read a book and she spent much of her time reading to us.

She was an excellent reader and she chose passages that whetted our appetites. There were adventure stories; Jack London, Kipling, Thoreau for the boys, and love stories for the girls, always followed by an exchange of comments.

There was even poetry. Not Longfellow or Swinburne, but poets like Vachel Lindsay or Robert Service...

"Fat black bucks in a wine barrel room,

barrel house bucks with feet unstable,

reeled and roared and pounded on the table

hard as they were able..."

"I saw the Congo cutting through the black,

cutting through the jungle with a golden track,

and all along the river bank a thousand miles,

tatooed cannibals danced in files..."

Hell, before that class was over we were all prancing around the room chanting, "Boomlay Boom."

Miss Lorry even got us interested in writing. Instead of the horrible theme topics of past years; things like, "What I did last vacation," or "The Beauty of the Sunrise," she told us to write of what we knew so she could put it in her book someday.

Those she liked she read aloud to the class:

"How to Skin a Skunk Without Getting Polluted"

"How Old Man Torault Wrestled the Buck"

"How to Make Saffron Buns"

"My Father May be Head of the House,
    but My Mother is the Neck that Turns the Head"

That sort of thing....

Why, we even wrote poetry of sorts, usually couplets or limericks. They didn't have to be very good, but they had to rhyme like:

"Eino and Aili went to the well,
But what they did there I better not tell."

Or

"When my old man takes off his socks,
We plug up our noses with a bunch of rocks."

Still, Miss Lorry encouraged more noble sentiments. Once, I remember, when we entered her composition class, she was dressed as a member of a Sultan's harem.

"Shh!" she said softly. "Today I'm going to play you Victor Herbert's 'Natoma, The Dagger Dance'. You will watch and listen and then write down your thoughts and feelings about what happens."

She cranked up her Victrola and the music flooded the room while she danced, a wild eerie performance ending with that last vicious stab in the breast with a real knife. We screamed and wept until she rose from the floor and showed us that she was all right.

"Now write for me," she said, and left the room to change her clothes. Shaken, we did our best.

You must remember that this all happened more than 50 years ago in a very isolated little village in the deep woods of Michigan's Upper Peninsula.

Living there was surviving. No one had any money to amount to anything. Nothing new ever happened. There was no television, no radio - just gossip. Everything was known "about everyone-by every one." Horses and cows, meat and potatoes, fish and hunt, hang out the laundry and bake the bread, live and die; every day - every month; the seasons held no surprises.

With Miss Lorry's coming there was suddenly something new to talk about and oh, the cackling that went on. Nosy old Aunt Lizzie was the worst. She collected every choice morsel of Miss Lorry's daily doings, stopping kids on their way home to quiz them and to cluck with outraged shock at what was going on.

Finally, just before Christmas. she went to the superintendent and told him that Miss Lorry must go, that she was a bad influence on the children and the community, that half the highschool girls were shortening their skirts all the way up to three inches below the knee the way Miss Lorry wore hers. Some were even plucking their eyebrows. She continued interminably.

"They say she smokes in her rooming house and then hides it with perfume. And...Annie, the post mistress, says she got a parcel the other day that gurgled when she shook it so she probably drinks too. And she wears those red and orange dresses, with her legs showing even. Not proper for a schoolmarm that. And she reads dirty books and doesn't mind it if the boys say hell and damn in class. And what does she and those high school boys do when they go walking in the woods? Tell me that!"

Aunt Lizzie's sniffing grew louder. "I tell you she's a bad influence and she's got to be fired."

The superintendent didn't give in.

"Miss Young is the best damn teacher we've ever had come to town," he answered, "and you, my friend, are the nastiest old busybody I know. I'm running this school and I'll thank you to keep your evil thoughts to yourself hereafter."

But he told Miss Lorry about the confrontation and that she should know that they each now had a mortal enemy in Aunt Lizzie.

"Try to be as discreet as you can, Lorry," he begged, though he knew she couldn't be.

He was right. The next day Miss Lorry made a formal call on Aunt Lizzie, engaged her in very polite conversation and made her a present of a bottle of very fine wine. The gauntlet was thrown and accepted. Aunt Lizzie went to work in earnest, travelling all over town stirring up trouble, gossiping, spreading innuendo, inventing outrageous lies always prefaced by, "You know what I heard today? They say......!"

The more we tried to defend Miss Lorry the more certain some of our parents were that she had indeed made us her captives and was not a good influence. Our peaceful little village found itself divided in two camps and everyone was relieved when the Christmas holidays came and Miss Lorry took the train back to Boston.

My mother, who liked Miss Lorry very much and who had been greatly distressed by Aunt Lizzie's machinations, said she almost hoped that the teacher wouldn't return, though she would miss her greatly. She added that she doubted whether we would ever see Miss Lorry again.

She didn't know her woman. Miss Lorelie Young came back on the St. Paul train on New Year's Day, the day before school was to reopen. Three huge trunks came with her and the host of kids who met her lugged them up to her boarding house on their sleds in a triumphant procession.

Miss Lorry was back!

There was a steely look in her eye when she visited my mother that evening.

"Mrs. Gage," she said, "I almost didn't come back, but then I thought of those fine children and the terrible poverty of the lives of their parents and I knew I had to. I'm going to civilize this town, Mrs. Gage, or die trying. I'm going to bring it beauty; the arts, music, and the dance, and painting, and sculpture and drama."

My mother, who had had a gentle upbringing complete with finishing school, gasped and murmured something about Lady Quixote. Miss Lorry jutted her Yankee jaw.

"I'll make a beginning at least," she vowed. "You'll see!"

We saw.

She was a whirlwind of energy, a fountain of innovation. That was the liveliest winter our town ever had, before or since.

She put on some kind of program in the school gym almost every other week, begging us to make sure that our parents came to them.

She put on a lantern slide show of the great paintings of the world.

She held concerts "via Victrola."

She published a weekly town newspaper, all handwritten, with twenty copies made by us to be passed around from house to house.

She tried to organize a dancing club, offering to teach us how to waltz and do the fox trot.

She started a bridge club, complete with lessons, tables and refreshments.

She made an abortive attempt to create a mobile library, taking her own books to the homes of her students so that the parents might find one they would like to read.

She organized a barbershop quartet.

Miss Lorry failed, abjectly and completely. Everything she attempted ended in fiasco and frustration.

The lantern slide projector yielded only fuzzy gray ghosts of the pictures she so wanted to share with us - And besides, Mullu Ysotalo came reeking of skunk and a helluva fight ensued before Charley Olafson, the town marshal, stopped it. He went through his usual routine of simply picking up the participants, one in each hand, and banging their heads together. Charley was an artist at head knocking. Said he could "tell by the tonk" when he'd banged 'em just right. But the session was a shambles and Miss Lorry wept. All who attended the soiree said they had a fine time.

After the first concert, despite her enthusiastic interpretation of the classical music that emerged from the scratching old Victrola, few parents returned. In fact, Aunt Lizzie was the only one that did and she was there to hunt for trouble.

In desperation Miss Lorry shifted from records to home talent. She had discovered somehow that Old Three Toe Jack could play the violin and Bill Shipley the bugle and somebody else the harmonica. I played the flute, a cracked old wooden monster that took so much air that I was always dizzy after two minutes of coping with the leak. We also had vocalists and the barbershop quartet. All of us had planned to rehearse several times before the announced concert, but one rehearsal was enough to scotch the project.

Miss Lorry learned that the only tune Three Toe Jack could play was "Turkey in the Straw" and that he had no sense of rhythm at all.

Bill Shipley had a busted lip from a fight at the saloon and he couldn't hit more than a few notes of "Taps" on his battered old bugle.

The barbershop quartet came thoroughly plastered. One was so drunk that the other three had to hold him up; the vocalist flatted and the harmonica player was so nervous that he kept sucking in when he should have blown out. Miss Lorry was devastated.

Her weekly newspaper was a hit at first. Complete with items like: "Bill Mager says his horse hurt his leg skidding pulp yesterday" and "Church services will be held in the M.E. Church, Sunday at 11," (which everyone knew anyway), it even contained an extensive article on the Pyramids of Egypt by Miss Lorelie Young herself.

The paper died after three issues because it became obvious that there wasn't anything new in town and nothing in the paper, except for Miss Lorry's articles, that everyone didn't know about already.

The only adult who came to her bridge lessons was Old Lady Viehema, the Holy Jumper. She stormed in with an axe and a torrent of Finnish, smashing the tables and denouncing the entire affair as the work of Satan himself. She had eyes of fire and all of us, including Miss Lorry, fled.

Perhaps Miss Lorry's biggest dissapointment was her dancing club. Surely, she thought, her devoted boys and girls would enjoy learning to waltz and fox trot. The girls showed up, but not a single boy came.

My mother helped her understand.

"You see, Lorry," she said in her soft voice, "It isn't that they don't want to come. It's that they don't have shoes. Haven't you noticed that they wear their swampers, those rubber bottomed boots, always? A few have moccasins for summer, but those boots are all they have and it would be pretty hard to dance in them."

The trouble, though my mother didn't mention it, was deeper rooted than that. Miss Lorry just didn't understand that everything always stopped during the long bitter winter. We didn't leave the house any more than we had to. Forty below and four or five feet of snow on the level and mountainous drifts had conditioned us to hibernation like the bear and the others of the seven sleepers. You conserved your energy all you could and waited for spring so you could change your underwear. At the time of the long sleep Miss Lorry's strange enthusiasm made little sense.

All of us felt sad to see the light go out of her eyes. She became thin and my mother would invite her to our house each week to give her a good meal and lift of spirit. My mother knew how she felt. She too had tried and failed many years before to find some fun in the bleakness of winter.

"Lorry," I remember her saying, "This is the time to wait. The Finns have a good word for it - "sisu" - the ability to endure anything. This is the time of the long night. Try again in the spring and everything will be different. But sisu now."

Miss Lorry finally took her advice and confined her energies to planning and writing the musical comedy that was to be the highlight of her sojourn with us. She scheduled the show for the week before the end of school, the first week of May.

Our school ended earlier than most because the boys had to help plant potatoes and that was when the walleyes and northern pike were spawning in the rivers. We had to fill the fish barrels for marinating and salting down or smoking and do our beaver trapping if the snows lingered.

Miss Lorry finished her musical about the end of March and all of April was spent learning the songs and lyrics and rehearsing and making costumes.

It was good to see her come alive again and her enthusiasm fired us all. A real live show just like they had in the big city -
Singing and dancing,
Chorus girls,
Her Magnum opus,
Her last gallant try...

Oh, how hard we worked making the sets, rehearsing lines and lyrics until they were letter perfect, making the signs that advertised the play, sewing the costumes.

I don't know how much money Miss Lorry spent, but it must have been considerable, far more than the miserable salary she got from the school board.

I remember how she and my mother made the sewing machine hum night after night, putting together the golden panties the chorus girls would wear, a task Miss Lorry didn't dare farm out to their mothers lest all hell break loose. You must remember that none of those loggers or farmers or miners had probably ever seen a live show or a line of chorus girls come kicking out of the wings. That chorus line was to be the final number, the grand finale. We were sworn to secrecy and we never told a soul.

Tickets were free, but we made them and covered the countryside passing them out and explaining what they were for. The show was called "Out Where the West Begins" and it has cowboys and Indians and a love story and fine music. That's what we told them. An event!
"Going show?"
"Yah."

The school gymnasium was overflowing, balconies and all, with people sitting on the steps that led down to the basketball floor on that "night of nights."

Never had there been such a crowd in the place. Everybody was there, even old shaggy Arne Nevola from Horseshoe Lake. There were trappers and lumberjacks that no one had seen for years.

Even though everybody had had their spring bath, the place stank with hot crowded bodies and the bear grease on the shoepacs.

Finally the fanfare came from the Victrola in the wings and the curtain went up. You could hear Charley Olafson sniffing and grunting as he cranked it off stage.

Out marched a mixed chorus to the recorded strains of "Mademoselle from Armentiers." They were garbed as soldiers returning from the war. Back and forth they marched across the stage singing, "Over There," but with Miss Lorry's words, ending with "It's good to be back from being over there."

Very stirring.

Applause.

Then a dramatic scene in which the heroine, in nurse's costume, tells her parents that she can't settle down now that the war is over, that she's leaving home again, leaving to go west, to The Frontier.

From the wings the chorus bellows loudly, "How you Gonna Keep Em Down on the Farm Now that they've Seen Paree?"

The curtain comes down as our heroine bids her parents farewell. Loud clapping.

And Gascon Barbassou, one of those who had seen Paris during the late war, gets up and yells from the back row, "Sacre Mo Jee, she's right, mes amis. It hard to come back to ze bush wen you see Paree."

Laughter.

The next scene opened with the chorus dressed as lumberjacks and miners singing, "Out Where the West Begins." All I can remember of the lines -

"Where cows meander the streets complacent,
Where all the movies are wild and ancient,
Where the doctor kills every other patient..
That's where the west begins."

We sang it loud and clear and everyone in the audience nudged his neighbor and looked at the doctor, my father. When he threw back his head and laughed too, the crowd went into uproarious clapping and One-Eye Foulin hollered from the back -

"Yah, and them cows they sheet all over the sidewalk too."

Ah, we had grabbed the audience.

It was going to be a success!

From the wings came the sound of chopping and sawing as the chorus disappeared. Out staggered a lumberjack covered with ketchup and pseudo blood, moaning loudly. Enter our heroine, the nurse, to minister unto him, bandaging his wounds, wiping up the ketchup and singing some song of comfort.

Some old lumberjack hollers from the audience, "Hell, put some tobacco juice on it and he'll be all right!"

Great gales of laughter.

I forget much of the rest. There was a barroom scene with a painted woman doing some eloquent bumps and grinds on a table while the chorus sang, "Every Little Movement Has a Meaning of Its Own," and which ended in a helluva realistic fist fight, complete with authentic black eye for Sulu Virta, and an Indian being tramped on the sawdust floor.

Again our nurse appears, does her good deeds, heals the hurt and reproaches the roisterers for their evil ways in a song entitled, "Drink is E-vil," followed by another chorus of "Out Where the West Begins," whereupon Billy Bones, our town drunk, takes a snort from his bottle and passes it around to his friends in the balcony.

"Yeah," he shouts down, "Drink is E-vil to be sure, but Wahoo!"

That rotgut whiskey he bought for a buck a pint down in Wasek always made you yelp!

Then there was a moving love scene in which Howard Lemond and the nurse sang to each other tenderly. It ended with a clinching embrace into which Howard threw himself so enthusiastically that our heroine, Millie Lapin, howled with pain and yelled, "Howard, you hug like a bear! Let me go, you bastard!"

The lines weren't in the script, but they brought down the house Out Where the West Begins!

Then came the final scene, the Grand Finale, the one all of us had kept secret for so long. All the characters on the stage were singing. Out from the wings came the pony chorus, girls linking arms and kicking high in unison. Lots of bare leg below the short golden panties.

Wahoo!

Uproar.

From the front row of seats, most of which had been taken by his wife and eleven children, jumped Pete Floriot, his eyes bulging.

In a voice that shook the building, he roared, "Maggie! Have some decent! Cross yer legs below!"

He had spotted his daughter, Marguerite, kicking high.

Outraged, Pete leaped to the stage, grabbed the weeping girl, gave her butt a resounding swat and yanked her down over the footlights, through the aisles and up the stairs. You could hear his voice giving her French hell until the front door of the school slammed shut.

Catastrophe!

The chorus line was broken, the girls were in tears, confusion was everywhere.

The air was electric, like it always is just before a good fight breaks out.

But out of the wings swept Miss Lorry, her head held high.

"The show must go on!" she shouted, and go on it did. Inserting herself in Maggie's place, she danced them off and then back in again, kicking higher than any of the girls.

Defiantly!

Proudly!

The whole ensemble sang the theme song lustily and the curtain came down - Out Where the West Begins.

61

That night the school board met in executive session and fired Miss Lorry. No formal charges were presented, but everyone knew what Aunt Lizzie had long suspected. Miss Lorry didn't wear any panties under her skirts and she had kicked too high and too revealingly.

As one of the board members succinctly put it, "You just can't teach here after you've shown the whole town yer twat!"

Miss Lorry departed on the train the next evening and all of the kids and half of the town's adults were there to see her off. As the train pulled away from the station most of them were weeping as Miss Lorry waved from the back of the sleeping car... But I'm sure that what she remembered most was that we sang to her - "Out Where the West Begins."

REDHANDED

For many years no one in our village ever locked the doors of a house at night or even when the family left for several days at berry picking time. The possibility that evil persons might enter our houses or barns to take something that didn't belong to them never entered our heads. If we shut the gates of our barnyards it was only to keep our cows inside or someone else's cows or horses out.

Oh, you might shut the doors of the chicken coop tight, but that was because of the skunks and foxes. There were plenty of odd people in our town and, after their fashion, a lot of sinners, but no thieves.

"You don't take nothing that don't belong to you," was drummed into every child's head as soon as he could listen.

I suppose this community-wide honesty was partially the result of our village's isolation and smallness, for surely there's a bit of thievery in all men.

It was just that if you took something, you couldn't use it anyway for everyone would know instantly who it had belonged to. And besides, most of us were poor and we knew very vividly how difficult it would be to replace something that was stolen. When you had to wage the battle of survival yearly, when you had to scheme and scratch to make it through the next winter, you just couldn't take away the tools or things that your neighbor needed to help him do the same. If you needed a particular tool all you generally had to do was ask to borrow it - and make sure it was returned in better condition than when you got it.

Then too, since all of us were in about the same boat as far as possessions were concerned, there was very little envy. If your neighbor had a better pair of skis or a bigger stack of wood than you, he had gotten them by his own labor and you could have them too if you wanted to work badly enough. If we had any real unsatisfied wants, they were not for things, but for opportunities - like for a chance to do more hunting and fishing!

Anyway, that's how it was in our forest village until the Trader came to town and moved into one of the company houses that had been vacant since the iron mine closed. Jim Olson, caretaker for the mining company, said the Trader had signed the year lease under the name of Mordecai Jimson, paid his twelve dollars and agreed to repair the house as required.

The mining companies owned all the land on which our town was located. You could buy one of their houses or build your own and the annual lease-rent was very cheap, but you couldn't buy a bit of the land since the company hoped to reopen the mine someday. Or so it was said.

This arrangement did have some advantages. For example, if some undesirable character came to town or someone didn't keep his place up, the lease was simply not renewed and he had to move out. We always sized up any newcomer by watching to see how he fixed his place up.

The Trader sure did. For a month he worked like a beaver on his house and barn. He even painted the windowsills and doors bright red when he got everything else done. Finally he started trading. He'd drive into your barnyard with his long wagon, one with a big box on top, knock at your backdoor to ask if you might be having some old jug, copper bottom boiler, tools or junk that you might like to trade for what he had. Always polite and sweet talking was the Trader.

Since it was kind of hard to resist taking a look at what he had in the wagon, you'd usually find something in your house or barn that you didn't really need and then the Trader would open the padlock on the long box and let you take a look. He always had quite an assortment of things in there, nothing new, but all carefully repaired or in good shape - tea kettles, hammers, axes, a couple pairs of boots, a shovel or two, all kinds of things, even toys.

Anything he had that was made of wood or metal was always painted the same bright red as the trim on his house and barn. Sometimes the things in the box looked better than they really were, but generally most of us felt we'd gotten the better end of the swap.

The Trader would usually haggle just enough to make it interesting, but usually he'd give in and you'd feel good getting a sound 10 gallon crock, maybe, for that old broken rocking chair that you were going to chop up for kindling anyway. It was really kind of exciting to have the Trader come to your house.

I remember that once I got a pretty fair jackknife in exchange for some empty Mason jars that we had discarded because the meat in them had spoiled. Sometimes, if you didn't think you had anything to trade he'd ask if he could take a look at your barn or shed to find something he wanted so he could make an offer and, of course we always let him.

I don't know how long it took after the Trader came to town before we began to suspect that he might be a thief. Quite a while, if I reckon right. The first things we began to miss were from our hunting camps: a bucksaw, a coffee pot, a blanket or two.

In those days, no one ever locked his hunting camp either and anyone was free to use it when the owner wasn't there. We also left our cabins stocked with a few cans of beans, coffee, sugar and hardtack so that anyone who was lost or who needed a snack before making it back to town could help himself. It was sort of an unwritten law of the woods. But none of us would ever take anything away from a hunting camp and certainly not the kinds of things that began to disappear. You just didn't take axes or coffee cups or frying pans. At first, the men suspected that some of us kids were furnishing one of the many shacks we were always making, but they looked them over and concluded that we weren't.

Then other things began to disappear too, from our barns and sheds and even our houses. It might be a rake, shovel, even a crowbar or perhaps only a file.

The set of Victor mink traps that Arne Ysamaki had boiled one evening and hung up on the sauna to dry was gone the next morning. A whole row of Pere Moulin's potatoes had been dug up overnight. When cutting marsh hay down in Beaver Dam Swamp, Eino Sonninen had left his rake and pitchfork on the haycock Saturday night as he had every summer for years. On Monday morning they weren't there. Another time 'Sier Broussard's sledge was missing. Mrs. Salo's cow, newly freshened after the calf was born, had been milked almost dry between morning and evening right out in the clearing back of the grove. Some dried fish hanging on the back of Antila's shed disappeared. A length of chain left outside the blacksmith's shop was gone. There were many happenings of this sort.

It was bad. When one of the French Canadians down in the valley had something taken, he blamed it on some Finn up on the hill and vice versa. Neighbors began to watch each other's kids suspiciously. After they turned out their kerosene lamps at night, people stayed awake as long as they could, peering out of their darkened windows.

In one month, M.C. Flinn sold more of his old padlocks than he had in twenty years.

Arne Hutilla left a new pitchfork sticking out temptingly from the hay-cock next to his barn and set two bear traps under some straw beside it, but all he caught was Piiku's big hound dog.

Charley Olafson, our constable and night-watch, almost went crazy checking out the complaints.

"When I ketch that varmint I'll bang his bloody head on a rock," he threatened and he would have too. Charley was big, but he was slow and not just slow afoot either. He was very good for banging heads together to set-tle fights of for hauling drunks up to the cage in the Town Hall to sober up, but not much for detective work. We sure had a lot to talk about that sum-mer and winter, but it was mostly bad talk. Too much suspicion hung in the air.

We gradually began to discern a pattern in the thieving. It usually hap-pened at night and more in the summer. In the winter things were stolen only when we had a bad blizzard to cover the tracks. Every so often we would have a spell when nothing was taken. I don't know who it was that noticed that these times seemed to coincide with the Trader's occasional ab-sence. You see, about once every month or six weeks, he'd take a trip to one of the other towns in the vicinity and be gone for a week and then return with fresh trading stuff in the long box.

Some had been suspicious of him right from the start, he being a new-comer in town and having had the chance to look over our premises, but since he seemed like such a nice, honest sort of man, people hated to air their suspicion out loud. Nevertheless, once spoken, it became almost a certainty. The Trader must be the thief. It made sense.

"Bet that barn of his, the one he keeps padlocked all the time, is just full of our stuff," someone said at the post office.

"Yeah," said another, "and then he takes it to the other towns and trades it there, steals their stuff and trades it here."

"Yeah, and fixes it up and paints it red to keep anyone from finding out," added a third man.

People began to wonder how much of the stuff we'd gotten from the Trader actually belonged to someone else in our village. We somehow hated to use any tool painted red because anyone who had lost one like it would be sure to come and look it over.

Pitu Angeaux, for example, was sure that the red hammer his neigh-bor Marcel DeForet had traded for was the one taken from his wagon one night.

"Me, I know by ze heft. Eet was ze only hammair I ever have I like," he said. But he couldn't prove it.

As you can imagine, we watched the Trader pretty carefully from then on and although the thefts continued, they weren't quite as frequent.

There were also some who tried to visit him when he was working in his barn, but the Trader always refused to let them in. He even got kind of nasty about it and nobody ever got to see the inside of his house. He told those who tried that they should mind their own business same as he minded his.

When he went on one of his trading trips, even around the village, every door of his house and barn was double padlocked and the curtains were always drawn. The Trader had the only barn in town that had curtains on the windows.

Someone asked him about it once and he answered again, "None of your business, but that's my workshop where I repair the lousy stuff you people stick me with when I trade with you."

Kind of surly, he was.

As you can imagine, the town soon soured on the Trader once the suspicion took hold and he began acting the way he did. People refused to let him bring his wagon into their barnyards. They wouldn't trade or let their kids trade either. Some even called him thief to his face.

Finally, Jim Olson, the mining company caretaker, went up to see the Trader and told him that he'd have to clear out, that his lease would not be renewed and warned him of bad trouble that was brewing.

"Whether you're our thief or not, Trader," he said, "you'd better get the hell out while you can."

The man nodded and said he reckoned he'd have to. He'd have to get his things together and probably have to make three or four trips. He planned to go to some place up the line where people weren't so god-damned evilminded, he said.

When the news of the Trader's impending departure spread around town, the response was more anger than relief.

"That son-of-a-bitch is a-going to cart away half our belongings," said Olie Anderson angrily. "Are we going to let the bastard get away with it?"

Wiser heads counseled good riddance and there probably wouldn't have been any violence at all if Mrs. Murphy's pet pig hadn't been taken the very next night. Some still say it was a bear, and the way the pig pen had been shambled it could well have been, but whatever it was, it triggered off a real doings.

A bunch of men just walked up to the Trader's house that next evening after dark, busted in his door, took him and put him in his outhouse and nailed the door shut. Then they shot the padlock off the barn door, took everything out of it, spread it in the yard, and did the same to everything in the house, beds, blankets, curtains - even the stove. Setting a guard to make sure the Trader couldn't get away, they passed the word around the village to come next morning and claim anything that had been stolen or missing.

Well, come daylight you'd have sworn there was an auction going on there in the yard. People were scurrying around and looking everything over and talking like sixty. Only Charley Olafson, our constable, was absent. He was too sick to carry out his duties, but to look close for a pipewrench with a nick in the handle.

That pipewrench wasn't found in all that display of things in the Trader's yard. What's more, there were only a few people in the crowd who felt strongly enough that something was theirs to take it away.

"Oh, old Lemisaari claimed that the red hayrake was the one that had been stolen from his shed and he showed us where the Trader had fitted in a new peg before painting it. And Pete Lafollete took away some traps that were his, pointing to where one side of each had been filed away, the place where he had always put his notch. There were a lot of people who thought they recognized something that belonged to them, but it had either been painted or repaired or dented in such a way as to keep them from being certain. It's hard to tell one camp frying pan from another. So, to their credit as honest folks, they couldn't bring themselves to claim something they thought 'might' be theirs. They just weren't sure enough. You would have thought they couldn't have acted so noble, but it wasn't so much being noble as their long habit of being honest. In our north country you just didn't take anything that didn't belong to you.

When the crowd dispersed at last, the Trader's yard was still plumb full of all sorts of things. The men who had run the whole show were plenty frustrated. They didn't have a shred of guilt though... They were sure they'd done the right thing. Everybody who had come that morning was still convinced that the Trader was the thief, even if he had been smart enough to alter and disguise the appearance of the things he'd stolen so much that their true owners couldn't recognize them.

People were really frustrated and mad until someone came up with the idea of painting everything red as a reminder that the people of our village weren't to be trifled with.

They put red paint on the horse's back and on the Trader's wagon and on the stove and chairs and tables and blankets and curtains, on every single thing that wasn't already painted. When everything from a coffee cup to an undershirt was daubed with at least one big splotch of scarlet, they opened the outhouse door and dragged the Trader into the yard. There they painted his shoes, then his hair and finally his hands. And then they all went home and had a very satisfying cup of coffee.

About a year later we were talking about the Trader and my father summed up the whole affair pretty well.

"No," he said to my mother, "I'm still not certain that the Trader was our thief. If he had been more people would have been able to claim their stuff, but, whether he was or not really doesn't make too much difference now. What happened to him sure made it mighty clear once again that you don't take anything that doesn't belong to you. Far as I know there hasn't been a thing taken from anyone since he left. Why, the kids didn't even swipe any of the apples from our trees last fall, and that's the first time they haven't since we've lived here."

OLD NAPOLEON

My father discovered the lake that now bears our family name in 1901. He said he'd gone deer hunting for the first time in his life, had gotten lost and was heading southwest when he cut across some huge tracks and decided to follow them a little way.

"Big as the hoof prints of a two year old heifer," he'd said. "Big as your hand."

The tracks led him north, over a hardwood hill where he'd jumped the buck, but he never got a shot.

"I saw him clear," my dad would say. "Looked as big as a horse and he had a rack like a brushpile."

Dad named that buck "Old Napoleon" and spent the rest of his life trying to shoot him.

Of course no deer ever lived as long as my father who died at the age of 94, but in every forest area there is usually one gigantic buck, wise enough and wary enough to become part of the legend of "Old Napoleon."

I've seen an Old Napoleon four or five times in some thirty years of hunting and I've seen his tracks much more often. I can understand my father's obsession with that majestic animal.

And an obsession it was, almost of the nature of Ahab and Moby Dick. Dad thought and talked about Old Napoleon every week of the year - even when he was trout fishing and e-v-e-n when they were biting. No matter how many deer he killed, and he shot a lot of them, the end of each deer season left him with a profound sense of respectful outrage. Old Napoleon had outsmarted him again.

Dad always returned from deer hunting with a tale of another encounter.

One year Napoleon had circled the camp at night, coming close enough to look in the cabin window.

Another time dad retraced his steps after lunch and found clear evidence in the fresh snow that Old Napoleon had followed him to the knoll where he was sitting, had watched and pawed the ground not thirty yards away.

One year, standing on the ridge at the end of the escarpment, dad heard the big buck coming right toward him - crunch, crunch, crunch - breaking the new snow crust, getting closer and closer in the heavy brush to the little clearing where the gun could cover well enough to shoot. And then a damned red squirrel had sounded off in a maple right above dad's head. A long silence - then crunch, crunch, crunch - the big buck back-tracked and got away, leaving nothing but his huge footprints behind.

Another year, dad said he almost had him again. He came across Old Napoleon's tracks at the edge of the forest opening we called Beaver Clearing. It's an odd place with a big bluff surrounded by a few acres of open plain through which a small spring creek meanders. The big buck had crossed the swale and bounded up the bluff. Cautiously, dad had made enough of a circle to see that no tracks descended on the other side.

What to do?

Where to sit or stand?

Dad finally decided to follow the tracks up to the base of the bluff and then to run, as fast as he could around its side, hoping to get a shot as the deer came down.

Dad did all this.

Nothing stirred.

Not a sound.

Finally, he went back to where the buck had climbed the bluff, the only easy place to get up, and there he found Old Napoleon's tracks coming down.

"Walking!" my father had said with rueful admiration.

"That old buzzard had been watching me all the time. Walking! He was probably watching me all the time. And probably laughing at me. I'll get him next year."

That year he'd found Napoleon's bed in some cedars just north of the lake, still warm and steaming in the frosty air, but the tracks showed no alarm. They also showed that the buck was feeding as he strolled, a cluster of huge prints revealed how he had reared to reach an especially succulent looking sprig of cedar ten feet from the ground. With his heart pounding in his ears, dad had tip-toed down the fresh trail, finger on the safety, ears and eyes straining. The tracks led into a big blow-down of fallen spruce, miserable stuff for a man to make his way through though the big buck had leaped the windfalls easily.

When dad was halfway through the tangle, Old Napoleon snorted, so near and so loud that dad said he almost fell off the log he was balancing on. Again the buck snorted. And again.

As dad said, "The old devil had me right by the balls. He knew exactly where I was and try as hard as I could, I couldn't spot him. And he circled me, snorting every minute or so while I stood there frozen on the windfall. Finally Old Napoleon was back there by his bed where I'd come from and he gave me one last big blast and took off in bounds that were twenty feet across. I suppose he had to get back there before he got wind of me, but oh, those were some of the longest minutes I've ever spent. I'll get him yet. I'll get him next year."

That year dad vowed to get Old Napoleon or bust. He'd hunt no other deer. He'd run him down. He'd follow his trail till hell froze over. When my father came back that year he was chastened. He told us that he hadn't even seen the big buck's track till the day before they had to break camp, but then he'd taken off after him, trailed him from nine in the morning until almost dark.

Dad had returned to camp, got some food and a blanket, returned to the trail and slept beside it until dawn. Then he took up the chase again.

"Lord, what a rounder," dad said. "Old Napoleon led me east to the Oxbow, then northwest around to the third lake, then over to Rock Dam, then back not fifty yards from the cabin. I think he was trying to tell me something. Saw him twice, but never got a shot. I'm bushed right down to the bone, but I'll get him yet. I'll get him next year."

And so the tales went - year after year.

Looking back, it seems as though Old Napoleon became almost as much a part of my life as of my father's.

In my childhood, the opening of the November deer season was as exciting as Christmas or the Fourth of July.

The week before was spent in preparation, gathering supplies, targeting the rifle, cleaning it, polishing it, hearing the tales of big bucks again and again.

In the kitchen, the baking was going on and butter was churned for the big crock. The big hampers were filled with Hudson Bay blankets and the foodstuffs were checked off against 'The List.'

I still have 'The List,' though the writing is faded: One bushel of potatoes, two slabs of bacon, one ham, sixteen loaves of bread, flannel nightshirt, extra compass, handaxe... and fifty other items.

Then the great day would finally come. Dad's four hunting cronies assembled - Cap Keys, Lou Touloff, Swede Ackman and Tony Marchetti, the tough Italian timber cruiser who could sling a deer as big as he was across his shoulders and carry it two miles.

They were all big men, stomping into the house in their red caps and red-plaid Mackinaws, gay and carefree as children unexpectedly let out of school.

Then up the street would come Pete Tario with his great brown horses pulling the lumber wagon or sleigh up to the back door. Then there was more joking and man talk as the hampers were loaded. Old Napoleon's name always danced around in the frosty morning air.

I remember running alongside the rig as far as I could, reminding dad that this was the year he was to come back with the big buck... He needed no reminding!

The years of my youth slipped past and I was finally granted the occasional privilege of driving the buckboard or cutter up as far as the bridge and walking over the hills to deliver a message or a packet of Chicago Tribunes to the cabin. I never did find my father there. He was always out hunting Old Napoleon, but the other men made me welcome. As they continued their poker game, they would tell me to help myself from the big stewpot on the box stove and invite me to admire their deer, already hanging from the buck pole outside. Big, rough men, they made me feel grown-up.

I never had the chance to join them, indeed to even go deer hunting, until many years later when I finally got a job that permitted me to take off that week in November. I always managed to get up to the old cabin for a short time every summer, however. I brought my young bride up there on our honeymoon and later led or lugged my children in in a packsack and I wandered the forest and lakeshore in July or August, always looking for Old Napoleon's tracks. One place or another, I always found them.

And dad, who sometimes joined us, would sit in the old rocker and retell the stories of the hunt.

As his old cronies died or grew too feeble to hunt, a few of my friends and I took their places in the cabin with dad in deer season. One year the bridge over the river went out in a great flood and hat-snatching alders gradually crept across the logging trail up which the teams had hauled the supplies. For some years we had to pack everything in, but the annual hunt continued.

In his seventies, dad hunted like a man possessed. At four in the morn-

ing he would begin clicking his watch-cover in the top bunk, turning on the flashlight to see if it was time to get up. He would always rouse us at five-thirty with his cry of "Daylight in the swamp! Today I get Napoleon!" And then we'd have to sit around after breakfast, waiting for daylight.

Dad was always the first to leave camp and the last to return. He rarely came back for lunch. We worried about him. He'd stagger in at dusk so exhausted and trembling so hard that he could barely hold the shot glass of whiskey to his lips. Sometimes he'd fall asleep in his chair, cleaning his rifle, and we usually had to help him up the birch ladder to sleep for an hour or two before the evening meal. At night the ache in his old bones would make him moan aloud in his sleep, but he could never wait to get going again next morning.

Napoleon, Old Napoleon! Without quite saying so, he'd made it clear that the great buck was his alone and that no one else should shoot him.

None of us would have.

We got a lot of spikehorns those years of dad's seventies.

During that decade dad shot only one buck, though in other years he rarely failed to get both the camp deer and one to take home. He was a very good hunter.

Dad saw plenty of deer he could have shot, but he was after Napoleon. No other deer would do. I think he was 75 when he made that one mistake.

I worried about him and had made it a practice to trail him discreetly and so I was able to join him shortly after I heard the shot. He'd dropped a monster buck, 280 pounds at least.

"You got him, Dad. You got Old Napoleon!"

My father shook his head.

"No, no," he said. "It's a good buck, but just a baby compared to Old Napoleon. Look, only sixteen points and look at these tracks. Not half big enough. Well, I'll get him next year."

He seemed depressed.

Lord, it was a big deer. I broke two ribs trying to lift it over a windfall on the way back to camp.

When dad was 79, he insisted that I take my 14 year old son, John, out of school so he could join us up at deer camp, so I bought the boy a gun and a license. In our state, a boy John's age could only hunt deer in the company of a supervising adult and dad insisted on taking over that role.

He filled the kid with so much hunting lore that I was afraid John would sicken and never want to hunt again. Moreover, dad was a stern task-master, impatient with hunting error.

Once, after the old man had given him bloody hell for moving his head before moving his eyes while overlooking a runway, John had become sullen and asked to hunt with me.

I said no.

The last day of the season he asked to go hunting alone and I let him take the trail up to Porcupine Bluff and hunt by himself. Dad didn't approve, but when he heard the two shots he was on the bluff almost as soon as I. And there the two of us shared that curious atavistic experience of watching a boy suddenly become a man. John was alternately elated and sober, excited and depressed. He insisted on cleaning the buck himself and on dragging it back to camp without any help from us.

From that time on he chopped the wood without being told, carried a bigger pack without protest and joined in our man talk around the stove.

Only recently did my son tell me that his grandfather had taken him down to the lake later that same day, told him that all that land would someday be his and confessed to the boy that his own hunting days were over.

"Maybe I'll not be able to get Old Napoleon after all," he told John. "I'm not the man I was, but if I don't get him, then by God, you do!" Then he swore the boy to secrecy.

The next year, when dad passed his eightieth birthday, for some utterly important reason that I now forget, I was unable to go deer hunting. Dad bought a license and made an attempt to walk up through the tangle that by then had completely covered the river road, but he got so worn out before he reached the place where the bridge had been that he barely made it back. For the first time he admitted that he was getting old. The next year we packed into the cabin and hunted, but it wasn't the same without dad. His rocking chair was always empty. No one wanted to sit in it. It was not a good deer season either. There were only a few small deer around and no sign at all of Old Napoleon.

After that we stopped coming up to the lake except in summer and then we portaged in by canoe from the west through the second lake, up the creek, over the beaver dam and finally into dad's lake. He didn't want to come with us. Too old, he said, too hard work, but over and over he expressed the wish to see his lake and the old cabin again.

When dad turned 92, my brother John and I decided to fulfill that desire. A new crop of loggers had cleared the river road, built a new bridge and were hauling pulp down from the headwaters. Knowing that the old man could never walk in, we hired some contractors to bulldoze, grade and gravel a new road to the lake. It cost us plenty and a lot more to build a fine new cabin on the rock point below the old cabin.

The old one was in really bad shape by this time. The bottom logs had rotted so much that we could only open the door part way and the inside was a shambles, thanks to the porcupines who had taken up residency and lived riotously for some years. Nevertheless, we had the men make a side road to it on the chance that dad might want to visit it again. My children and their children cleaned the old cabin up as best they could.

Dad was 94 when everything got done...just before deer season. By this time he was very frail and we were very upset to learn from his housekeeper that he had gotten himself a hunting license. He was polishing up his rifle between naps. When my brother, John and I arrived the week before the opening, we tried in vain to dissuade the old man.

"One last hunt," he said. "Got to get Old Napoleon. Just put me out on a log somewhere and let me be."

His voice quavered, but he looked us hard in the eye. So we brought up his things, got the new cabin warmed up, and scouted around for a good place beside the road where he might sit for a few minutes for auld lang syne and his ancient dream. I found a good spot overlooking the bend in the new road before it started up the hill, a place where a heavy deer trail crossed. And I wrestled one of the old camp chairs out of the cabin and put it in place behind a blind I'd built of branches. Sneakily, I scattered a few apples on each side of the road where the deer trail crossed. Dad would have shot me for doing it, had he known.

We brought him up the evening before season opened. He kept looking out the car window, watching for tracks in the inch of freshly fallen snow. Once he asked us to stop and back up to where a deer had crossed.

"Naw," he said, "That's just an old doe. A big one, but the toes are too pointed. Old Napoleon's tracks are bigger and blunted from long pawing the ground during rutting time."

He was excited and remained that way. His hands trembled so much that when he drank his tea at suppertime he had to use both hands to lift the cup. After the meal we sat him in the big chair in front of the fireplace and there he reminisced, telling of old days and good times in the old cabin.

How he and his cronies had once spotted a spikehorn through the window, trotting up the trail right toward camp and how three heavy men got stuck in the door trying to get out to shoot it.

And the night Touloff went out to take a leak and yowled like a lynx and had laughed at the rest when they'd run out in their underwear and bare feet to try to get a shot at it.

And the time dad painted Tom's huge nose a bright crimson with the newfangled mercurichrome dauber, telling him that it was a new cure for the sniffles and later that it would never wash off.

Or drawing a straw across the open mouth of a snoring bedmate and squeaking like a mouse.

And, of course, the tales of Napoleon.

The heat from the roaring fire and his cup of Old Crow finally put dad so sound asleep that he barely roused when we took off his boots and got him into bed.

We had already finished breakfast when the old man awoke at eight-thirty, but he still managed the old "Daylight in the swamp. Roll out, you buggers," cry. Too excited to eat much bacon and eggs, he let us help him on with his boots, fetch his old rifle and drive him up to the place I'd prepared. We had to help him walk over to the chair in the blind overlooking the deer trail. Then we bundled him in blankets and told him that whenever he had had enough or got too cold to just shoot his gun and we'd be right back to get him. When I left, dad was sighting down the rifle barrel at the deer trail. Somehow I almost wept. He seemed so frail and feeble.

I returned as soon as I'd taken the car back to the cabin, walking very carefully until I got to a little knoll where I could see dad and the deer trail very easily. I must have watched there twenty minutes before I heard a twig snap on the far side of the road where I'd scattered the first bunch of apples. I don't think the old man heard it, but a few moments later he certainly saw the huge buck that bounded across the road. He raised his rifle.

"Shoot! Shoot," I prayed silently. "He'll be in that brush. Shoot. Shoot now. Now!"

But the deer had smelled the other apples and began to feed on them broadside to my father, right in the open, not thirty yards away. Dad's rifle shook wildly as slowly, ever so slowly, he raised it up and I watched him steady it against the sapling that held up the blind.

"Shoot! Shoot! Now!"

I wanted to scream the words, but I couldn't.

The great buck suddenly looked up at both of us and the booming report of dad's gun echoed through the hills.

Old Napoleon didn't fall. Two magnificent bounds and he was out of sight and I knew why. Dad had raised his rifle and fired into the sky.

I made my way back to the road and joined my brother who had heard the shot. When we reached dad he just shook his head.

"You bundled me up too good," he said. "I must have dozed off for a moment and when I woke up there was Old Napoleon, going over the hill. I took a quick shot, but I missed. That derned old bugger outsmarted me again. I'll get him next year."

There was no next year.

But I vividly remember the little smile that crossed dad's face when he said it.

THE PADDYGOG

everal summers after my father's death, my daughter and her family were vacationing with me at his old house in the village where I spent my youth.

One morning, Jennifer, then eight, found me on the porch when she returned from playing with the village's current crop of youngsters.

"Grampa," she said. "We kids found a great big paddygog up there by the grove. What's a paddygog, Grampa?"

I had to confess that I didn't know, but that I would sure like to see one if she could lead me to it.

Up the old familiar street we went, hand in hand, Jennifer chattering all the way.

"It's awful heavy, Gramp, and big like this." She held her hands together in an arc above her head.

"And there's a big long chain on it and it's in the leaves by a big tree and it's kinda dirty, and that's what the other kids called it. A paddygog, Grampa."

She led me to the vacant space where our Town Hall stood before it burned down and then to a big maple tree.

"See! See! There it is, Grampa."

Jennifer pointed to a huge rusty iron triangle that lay half-hidden in the leaves and grass.

I recognized it immediately. It was Paddy's gong, the one he beat with a crowbar to celebrate the top o' the mornin' on St. Patrick's Day. It brought back a host of memories.

Patrick Feeny, Paddy as he was called by all the kids who adored him, was our village blacksmith.

My dad always claimed there were only two indispensible men in town: him, the town doctor, and Paddy, the blacksmith. The preacher and others were way down the list.

Dad fixed up the bodies.

Paddy repaired the things. He was not only a blacksmith, but a gunsmith and mechanic of great competence. He could fix anything from a watch to a broken logging derrick 30 feet tall. Moreover, his services were cheap. Paddy never set a price.

"Sure, and you can pay me what you think it's worth," he'd say. "Pay Paddy when you can."

That's how he operated and it was a shame how many people cheated him or didn't pay at all.

M.C. Flinn, the stingy old proprietor of our general store, probably took advantage of Paddy more than anyone else. Flinn used to say disapprovingly whenever his name was mentioned in connection with Paddy, "No way to run a business. No way to run a business." But Paddy never seemed to mind even when some of his customers complained about his being too slow.

He certainly worked terribly hard, not only in the smithy, but late at night in his home. Any evening a passerby could see him at the workbench by the front window, taking a gun or clock apart and putting it back together again. He especially liked clocks. His house was full of them. Said they kept him company. No one else did. People only came to see Paddy when they needed him.

But the smithy was his first love. I can see him yet, a huge man, built square to the floor from the shoulders down, in a sooty leather apron and ragged under shirt, his heavy hammer clanging a piece of white hot iron, fresh from the forge, until it turned cherry red. Then Paddy would plunge it hissing and smoking into the water barrel. It was almost as good as the Fourth of July to visit the blacksmith shop.

A single man, Paddy dearly loved children and always made us welcome though he'd built a bench back by the stanchions to keep us out of the way of sparks and bits of hot metal that sometimes shot from his anvil. Once in a while he'd even let us help pump the huge bellows on the forge until the fire roared, but we had to keep out of his way when he was shoeing one of the great draft horses the loggers and farmers brought in.

Paddy had a way with those horses. He'd lead them in, half crooning to them all the way till they were in place. Then he'd shove up his stool, take a monstrous hoof in his lap and start paring it with a knife as our eyes bugged out. The horses never seemed to mind a bit.

First he'd measure the hoof with big calipers then sort through a barrel for a new shoe, heating it red, bending it over the anvil. Then he'd cool it and nail it home with mighty blows, rarely more than two whops to a nail.

After the horse had been led away, Paddy would give us the hoof parings for our dogs or he'd save them for the trappers. They claimed you couldn't find better bait for wolves or coyotes than those parings.

Then Paddy would come over to our bench to give us a ginger snap from the big tin on the shelf, He'd pour himself a cup of tea and tell us wonderful tales of the wee people, the leprechauns of the ould sod of the Ireland he had loved, but left as a boy.

Like many powerful men, Paddy had a soft voice. His had a special "lilt to it" though, like he was talking music. This, along with his brogue, made us hang on every word lest we miss something.

He'd tell us gory tales of the wars between the old kings of Ireland from whom he claimed to be descended.

"Sure it is, me bhoys, that ivery Irishmon has a wee bit iv king's blood in him, that he has."

It was a little hard to imagine Paddy wearing a crown. His face was always so covered with soot that his eye holes gleamed white, but you could sure feel some hint of strange royalty just the same, especially when he told his tales about the slaughter of Shannon's Ford and stories of castles and dungeons. Paddy loved the land he'd left and he opened the windows of our isolated little world when he told of tinkers with high wheeled covered carts, long stone walls that curved across soft green hills and the smell of "taters" baking in the ashes of a peat fire hearth.

Perhaps it was because several generations had sat on that bench that no one

protested when Paddy went on his week long St. Patrick's Day spree.

At daylight he'd crank the chain that held the huge steel triangle that we called Paddy's gong down from the rooftree of the smithy. Then he'd take a sledge or crowbar to it till the reverberations woke half the town. I can hear the sound of it still, half boom and half clang, echoing from the hills that nestled our valley.

St. Patrick's Day!

Paddy Feeny was making sure that no one forgot the Irish.

But just the gong's great clanging flood through town wasn't enough.

Paddy always got out his big goose gun, at least an eight gauge with a barrel so big it was terrifying, and he'd shoot that off: first downtown, then in front of the post office and finally at the uptown post office. It sounded like someone had touched off a cannon! Everyone in the village knew then that it was St. Patrick's Day!

After he'd fired the goose gun, Paddy would visit old Mrs. Murphy. They'd have a cup of tea and talk about old times and maybe they'd sing a few Irish songs together. Then Paddy went to Higley's saloon, bought 10 bottles of rye whiskey and proceeded to get "polluted to the gills" for a whole week. Paddy never drank at any other time, but he sure laid a real drunk on then. He didn't do a lick of work either, just sang Irish songs or keened between bottles. Anyone who needed some iron work or horse-shoeing done made sure it was finished before St. Patrick's Day or they put it off till the week after. Year after year, Paddy "cilibrated" in the same way.

It was early February when people of the village suddenly realized just how important Paddy was to them and stopped taking him for granted.

He was doing something he'd done hundreds of times - fitting a huge steel rim on a heavy wheel from a logging wagon - and his knees just sagged and he fell on his face there on the brick floor of the smithy. Some men slid him onto a couple of boards and carried him over to his house while others ran for my father. The news spread swiftly through the village and dad had to shoo people out of the house before he could get to feel Paddy's pulse and put on the stethoscope.

"A massive heart attack," he concluded. "Go get the priest."

Unfortunately, Father Hassel had gone to Marquette that morning to see his bishop, but when he returned that evening, Paddy had rallied considerably. He still got the last rites and the lights of the Catholic Church burned all night as Masses were said for a soul that had seldom seen the inside of the confessional.

For three weeks Paddy lay abed. He received more attention then than he had in thirty years. He was never left alone for a minute. One or another of the neighbor women took turns hovering over him day and night. Dad said it wasn't so much their nursing as his digitalis and nitroglycerin that pulled Paddy through, but he was finally able to totter over to the smithy to offer advice to a strapping young lad who was clumsily trying to fill in.

"Now don't you let Paddy do a damn thing," my father warned. "He isn't even to lift a hammer. If he wants to sit on the bench with the kids for half an hour or so at a time, that's all right, but he's got to take it real easy for a long time or he's a dead man."

We made sure there was always one of us to sit on the bench with Paddy, but he didn't tell us any stories. He would run out of breath if he tried to talk very much.

Even after Paddy could get around, the townspeople made sure he was cared for. They cooked his meals, cleaned his house and watched over him constantly, showing in a thousand little ways how much they really cared. He couldn't even go to the outhouse without someone watching to make sure he came out again after a reasonable time. Paddy gradually improved enough to joke with the women about nagging him back to health.

According to dad, however, who examined Paddy almost every day, his apparent recovery was not a true reflection of Paddy's condition.

"Paddy's in bad shape," he told my mother. "I don't like what I hear in my stethoscope and his pulse is still none too regular. He could go anytime."

I sure felt bad when I heard him telling her that.

When the middle of March approached, the whole village began to worry again, especially after they heard that Paddy had sent Jim Pillion to bring his usual 10 bottles of rye from the saloon.

Dad blew his top, went over to Higley and read him the riot act for sending the whiskey and he tried to find it in Paddy's house.

"You drink half a bottle of that rotgut, Paddy, and you're dead. I tell you, you can't touch a drop of it. Now where did you hide it?"

But Paddy wouldn't tell.

"Now, Doctor," he said with that wide old grin of his, "a wee bit from the bottle nivver killed an Irishmon yet. An Irishmon will cilibrate the day, that he will, so long as he has a heart in him, will he not?"

Dad managed only to take away the goose gun.

"If Paddy tries to climb that hill, he'll be gone before he gets a quarter of the way up it," he told the neighbors. "And if he tries to take a sledge to that triangle gong of his, that'll do him in too. You watch him now. Paddy just can't do that kind of thing in his condition. I tell you he's got to take it easy for a long, long time."

But dad knew the nature of the Irish and he worried. So did the rest of the village.

I don't know who first got the idea, but I think it started in school. Some kid, probably a regular on Paddy's bench, thought that if we could hold a real slam bang St. Patrick's Day celebration in Paddy's honor the night before the day came, then he wouldn't feel he had to go through his old routine and kill himself.

"We'd cilibrate' for him."

The idea caught hold and grew so fast and spread so far that no one could stop it. My dad felt all the excitement might be more than Paddy could stand and he still worried.

78

"Well, I don't know," he told us at the dinner table. "It might just keep him from banging that gong and drinking that booze if he sees all of us sharing his Irish insanity. At least he'll find out that the whole town likes and respects him after all these years of neglect and Paddy's sure got that much coming. I just hope it won't hurt him."

Well, we really celebrated that St. Patrick's Day Eve and Paddy didn't even know that the whole doings were in his honor until he got out of Old Man Marchand's rig and entered the Town Hall.

It was full of people cheering him. It was full of green streamers and paper shamrocks three feet high. And it was full of Finns and French-Canadians, Indians, Swedes and "mixed stuffs," each with a bit of green on him to show he was Irish too. School kids were parading across the stage singing, "Where the River Shannon Flows" and other Irish songs.

And the speeches, too many of them, all telling Paddy how much he'd meant to the whole town. Old Mrs. Murphy was even trying to teach a bunch of little school kids how to do an Irish jig for him.

At the end of it all, Paddy was presented with a huge grandfather clock, a token of our esteem.

Paddy Feeny weathered it all and enjoyed every minute of it. After the clock presentation, he stood up, held out his arms to all of us and shouted, "Erin Go Bragh," and was driven home.

He went to bed and died in his sleep.

Everyone felt terrible, but the next day, St. Patrick's Day, the men hauled Paddy's big triangle up to the Town Hall, hung it by a chain to the roof piece and rang it till sundown. They rang it again the next year and on St. Patrick's Day every year after until the Town Hall burned down.

After my grand-daughter showed me her paddygog, I got a crew together and we hung the huge triangle from a big limb of the maple tree. Since Jennifer is half Irish, I lifted her up so she could be the first to bang it with a hammer and I gave each of the other kids a dollar so they would remember to ring it next St. Patrick's Day.

THE PROPHET

His name was Pierre Rousseau, but nearly everyone called him "The Prophet." Oh, there were some who called him fool and a few more who'd nicknamed him Paul Bunyan because of his enormous size, but they were all careful to address him as 'Sieur Rousseau or Prophet to his face.

Rousseau did indeed look like Paul Bunyan must have looked. Way over six feet tall and three feet across the shoulders, he was far and away the strongest man in our village, even stronger than the blacksmith. His bushy black eyebrows, full beard and a voice that rumbled like thunder in the hills had terrified me when I was a kid.

But The Prophet, like so many giant men, was gentle and easy going. He never fought in the saloon on Saturday nights and he never beat his wife, Minna, a tiny half-breed Chippewa who shared his cabin on a little farm out by the charcoal kilns northeast of town.

They had no children and that made The Prophet's heart ache for he loved them almost as much as he scared them... And he only scared them because he was so darn big and loud.

The first time I met him, I was about six years old. My dad and I were going into the post office to get the mail.

"Ah, my friend," he roared when he saw my father. "You 'ave a fine boy dere."

Then he bent down to give me a closer look and shouted, "Mon petit, you like to fly like a bird, no?"

I must have nodded as I shrank away because the next thing I knew he'd picked me up and thrown me ten feet in the air above his head. He caught me gently and put me back on my feet with a gale of laughter that sent echoes down the valley. I was terrified! I clung to my dad's leg until we got back to the horse and cutter and I had nightmares for weeks about a big black bearded monster coming out of my bedroom closet up there under the eaves.

"Tres formidable," was how the French Canadians described The Prophet!

The Prophet's predictions were legend in our town.

Once he'd foretold a great forest fire that would start in the Buckeye on August 14, and threaten our town - And it did!

There were some scoffers who'd said The Prophet had started the fire himself so the blueberries would be better the following year, but then there'd been the time he told Joe Hamel that his bay horse would die in the harness that day - And it did! And then The Prophet had nearly killed his own horse, racing half the night to warn Eino Ysitalo out by Wabik, one of his detractors, against going into the woods that day lest something evil happen to him. Of course Eino laughed and went anyway and, perhaps unnerved by the warning, had chopped a big gash in his leg. And another time he warned everyone against butchering their hogs after the second frost as they usually did. He said the meat would spoil. Those who failed to heed his advice regretted it too, because that was the first November that anyone could remember when not a single lake froze over and not a single snowflake fell.

The Prophet had made a lot of predictions and enough of them had come true that the townspeople now consulted him about the best time to make hay or when the pike would make their spawning run up the river or whether the M.E. church should have its Sunday School picnic on such and such a day.

Still, The Prophet knew his limitations. When Raoul Deforret, after fathering four daughters in a row, asked him to come and see his pregnant wife and tell him if he'd have another girl, The Prophet flatly refused.

"Women and cards, cards and women, women and cards...I don't perdick," he roared.

He specialized mainly in the weather.

Every day, except Sunday, The Prophet drove to town to give his weather prediction. He came to the post office at nine o'clock, just before the morning mail was "disturbed." You could hear him coming half a mile away, singing to his old mare Nanette at the top of his voice. She didn't seem to mind the singing as she pulled the wagon in summer or the sleigh in winter; rain, snow or shine. The Prophet had a lot of songs too; some English, some French, mostly both. The only one I can remember went something like.

"Oh ze wind she blow from ze nort'
And ze wind she blow som more,
But you want get drown on Lak Champlain
So long as you stay of ze shore..."

And everyday, as he entered the crowded anteroom in front of the mail boxes, a hush fell over the townspeople as they awaited the oracle's pronouncement.

"Ah, mes amis," The Prophet would begin, "You want for me to tell wot ze wethair will be, yes? Me, I say dat she will be..."

It was sort of like the "My broker is and he says that" commercial on modern television - except that The Prophet told them. No hedging either. No ten per cent chance of showers or snow flurries, or this or that, like they tell us today, but "It would rain that day, half a pailful; Or it would snow four and a half inch, oui!"

Then he predicted the weather for tomorrow and sometimes for a more extended time. It took a very brave or skeptical or foolish person to doubt him. The message seemed to come down from on high. From where I stood, it did!

The Prophet was remarkably accurate. Rarely did he miss calling the shots. Indeed, my father was so impressed by his uncanny ability to predict the weather that he made a trip out to his farm just to find out how The Prophet did it. He returned even more impressed.

"You know, Edith," he told my mother at the supper table, "The Prophet really studies the weather. He's got a real feel for science in a crude sort of way. I don't suppose he's ever heard about barometric pressure, but he showed me a marked stick - keeps it in his well - told me that when the water level went up that stick, even a little bit, that it meant rain. And he's got a whole woodshed full of calendars, thirty years worth of 'em, with notations for every single day. He told me he studied them and the clouds and the birds and a whole mess of other things before he made his 'perdickshuns'...'"

Anyway, we had no other source of information in our town during the first two decades of this century. There was no WLUC, no radio stations, no weather satellites... And the weather was important to us in a way that the modern city dweller would find hard to understand. A farmer or a fisherman might still understand, but most of you wouldn't.

Only a few families received a daily paper, The Chicago Tribune or The Mining Journal, and they were usually delivered several days after publication so the weather... had already happened.

So we appreciated 'our' Prophet's predictions. We believed them. And we relied on them. Through the workings of that curious communications grapevine that characterizes small villages, his weather news came to almost every house in town within an hour after The Prophet had spoken. Any discussion of the weather always began with, "Prophet says..."

All dogs have fleas, perhaps, as David Harum has suggested, "to keep them from brooding on being dogs."

Terry O'Hara was The Prophet's flea.

A feisty Irishman, barely five feet tall, aggressive, obnoxious and too small to hit, he heckled the giant unmercifully whenever one of his predictions didn't come true. He too was always at the post office when the morning mail came in, ready to rub it in. Even on the days when The Prophet's predictions for the previous day proved correct, Terry was there to yap at him.

He would pull out a small black notebook and read off past blunders in his little squeaky voice.

"And how about last Wednesday the fourth, big man? How about it now? Ye said it would rain, you did, and there wasn't enough rain to make a good spit."

The Prophet, towering above him, never answered. Once though, when Terry had gone too far with the spite of his tongue, The Prophet had picked him up with one hand, lifted him until he touched the ceiling and then quietly seated himself, dangling the little Irishman like a babe on his knee.

Only once in the 20 years of my adolescence did the people of our forest village lose faith in Their Prophet and they did a bit of crucifying... That always seems to be the lot of the seer.

It happened, if I remember correctly, in 1914-1915 or thereabouts.

The Prophet had stopped giving his daily and weekly forecasts, but concentrated instead on warning 'his' people about the terrible winter he saw coming.

Everyday in the post office, he would tell of the winter to come, of the miseries in store. It would be the year of 'ze long winter' - from October to June - it would snow - snow above the windows and be so cold that if you sneezed it would crack your nose.

"I tell you, my friend, make the wood, make the wood now or you run out by New Year. She's going blow an' she's going snow lak you nevair see before."

Terry O'Hara and his followers scoffed, but most families took The Prophet's warning seriously enough to build up their woodpiles, salt down an extra barrel of fish and smoke or can as much venison as they could get before the regular deer season came 'round.

The Prophet was really worried and showed it by divulging some new bit of weather predicting evidence each day.

The wasps had built their nests higher, much higher, off the ground. Ants were walking in straight lines instead of roaming around. A rooster had crowed at bedtime and the hen had moulted in August month. The milk-weed had opened its pods three weeks early. Northern Lights had been seen in July, way in the western sky too. The beavers had built their dams earlier and bigger than ever before. Squirrels were taking hazelnuts deep into their burrows instead of burying them in the leaves. The fish were not on the surface, but winter deep in the lake and the trout were already slimy in their spawning. The brown middle band of the wooly caterpillar was twice as wide as usual. A dry summer makes a deep snow winter. The lakes were open, but the geese had gone south.

"Buy a new suit of wool underwear," The Prophet suggested, "and grease your boots good."

All that warm, lovely September he preached his gloomy gospel, not just in the post office, but to almost every house in town - except O'Hara's.

The snow began to fall in the first week of October, just as The Prophet had predicted, and by mid-month there was more than a foot of it on the level.

"Start banking your house," The Prophet ordered. "Pile the snow high above the foundations. Get the hay-cocks out of the swamp and into the barn while you can. Forget the game wardens. Shoot your deer now. Butcher your pig and young steer. Cut some extra wood because it will soon be too late."

By the first of November, it was blatantly clear that The Prophet had been right.

Blizzard after blizzard roared down from Lake Superior, heaping snow in huge drifts. You could almost see it creeping upward to cover the tops of the picket fences. No one shoveled their walks except O'Hara and his looked more like a tunnel.

One of the trains got stuck in a great drift out by Red Bridge and you could hear its lonesome whistle calling urgently for help from the crew at the roundhouse by the station. The telegraph wires whined in the wind. Dogs, let out in the morning, floundered belly deep and were soon howling at the back door. Hoar frost so covered the door and window panes as the bitter cold clutched the houses, that the kerosene lamps were kept burning all day in the kitchens.

Waist deep, we tramped down a narrow trail to the outhouse and barn only to find it blown shut again within the hour.

With the schools closed, the sight of a man struggling up the street on skis, scarf over face and bending into the wind, was event enough to bring us all to the window. Only a few of the strongest managed to get to the store or the post office. Even The Prophet had been in only a few times on snow-shoes.

When he came, he reminded us of his prophecy in that voice like thunder. "Me, I tell you she's going to be a bad one. Like this till June, mes amis."

But toward the end of November the blizzards stopped.

It was still very cold, way below zero, but the sight of the sun at least gave us energy enough to stop huddling by the kitchen range and start living again.

Once the company team had compacted the four feet of snow on the street with the huge roller, Flinn's store bustled with people again as they replenished their necessaries. Every chimney lifted a tall exclamation point of white smoke into the cloudless, windless, cold blue sky. We had survived!

The fir trees still sagged with their burden of white, but the world seemed cleansed and bright again. Sometimes it was almost too bright... The surface of the vast drifts sparkled as though dusted with crystals of ground glass and the brilliance hurt our eyes so much that the children were given knitted face masks with slits to see through. But our spirits were high. We had survived. The worst had to be over. We'd never have a full month of storms again like those we'd just endured.

What was The Prophet saying now?

The news coming from the post office wasn't at all reassuring. Day after day The Prophet came, saying the same thing, that soon the snow would begin again, that the wind would blow again, that more storms were on the way, that winter would last until June. We began to hate our Prophet. The very thought of seven more months of frigid misery was just too much to bear. O'Hara' gained some companions in his giant badgering campaign.

But it came to pass just as The Prophet had foretold. December was bad; January was worse; and never before had February gone by without at least one short thaw.

The days limped along, each like every other, with snow, wind or both and a gray, gloomy sky. Our bones ached from the cold no matter how many sweaters we wore or how close we huddled to the open oven of the kitchen range. Depression seeped into and through all of us as fathers anxiously scanned diminishing woodpiles and mothers watched the Mason jars of meat and fruit disappearing from cellar shelves. No one left the house unless it was absolutely necessary. People stopped talking to each other --- even husbands and wives. The women cooked and knitted in silence; the men did the chores or just sat around, looking into space.

That was the winter I read the entire collected works of Charles Dickens - even "Martin Chuzzlewit" - hating every page of every volume, but having nothing else to do.

The horses in the barn, shaggy in heavy winter coats, refused to lie down on the cold floor no matter how much straw we put down in the stable. They locked their knees and slept standing up. The chickens stopped laying and the cows gave little milk. None of us even tried to scratch the frost from the window panes to see outside anymore. Even the sun, when it made a rare appearance, was ghost pale, not worth looking at.

Damn The Prophet, anyway!

We began to blame him for our woes.

We hardly cared to turn over the calendar when March came.

March - April - May - And The Prophet said we'd have snow in June.

Four more months of the same. Four more months to hunch down and sullenly survive.

But miracle of miracles, The Prophet was wrong!

It suddenly turned warm. The mercury climbed past the zero mark on the thermometer, then into the tens and the twenties. The days were cloudless, windless and the sun shone again. Over the barrier of 32 degrees inched the mercury.

"A little thaw," The Prophet said, but day after day the mercury rose further up the scale. It even stopped freezing at night!

By March 12th, we were having temperatures in the sixties. It was unheard of. Impossible. We always had terrible storms in March. Rarely did spring come until May.

We were almost afraid to hope and then the crows came back on St. Patrick's Day. Word of their arrival swept through the village like a crownfire in a spruce forest.

"The crows are back. No, not the ravens, the crows!"

We heard their ancient cry, a sure sign of winter's end.

No one who has not lived in the north country can possibly understand what the coming of spring can mean to those who have suffered the long cold, endured the bite of winter.

Oh, to watch the hill streets become rivers as great banks of snow sink and sag; To see the tops of fences again; To hear the great booming - shuddering echo across Lake Superior as the thick pack ice cracks and groans; To walk again down the railroad tracks on a Sunday afternoon; To walk, not to ski or snowshoe but to walk and without heavy clothing; To find the first patch of arbutus on a sunny bank; To catch that first sight of green grass!

The horses shared our exhilaration. Blinking and hesitant when first led from the barn, they were soon rearing and prancing or rolling over and over on the bare ground, kicking their legs in the air - just like we were. And the cows mooed and played bull with each other before munching the new grass so their butter would turn yellow again. Mrs. Haitema threw away the can of old coffee ground she'd been saving. Catholics went to early Mass again. The clotheslines blossomed with color all over town, long johns dancing in the breeze. Ponds, everywhere ponds, where we could sail little boats made from wood shingles, or wade, or just fall in and get soaked for the hell of it. Sparrows fought over fresh horseturds and boys fought over anything at all. Spring, Spring, Glorious Spring! We'd made it through the winter!

It was a tough time for The Prophet as you can imagine.

"What do you perdick today, Prophet? Snow till June, Prophet? Got your long underwear on yet, Prophet?"

O'Hara and his followers were in their glory.

Little children would run along beside The Propet's rig, chanting, "Prophet, Prophet, you're way off it" or You make us sick with I perdick." The big man ignored them mostly.

One weekend in early April, he predicted that a terribly heavy snow would cover the land the next Monday. He got the amount of precipitation right, but it was rain, not snow.

By the middle of the month the ground was dry enough to be plowed and potato planting began. Over and over, The Prophet pleaded with the men to wait at least until the usual time, Memorial Day, but by then the temperature was in the seventies, the pike had completed their spawning, violets and adder's-tongue and trillium were everywhere in the woods and it was summer-like. So they laughed at The Prophet and reviled him... so much that he stopped coming to the post office.

May came and the peonies bloomed in the yards. Maples shed their red buds and leafed out. Even the tamaracks in the swamps sprouted new green pinfeathers. By the third week of May, men were sharpening their scythes on the grindstones. It would soon be haying time.

The week before Memorial Day, The Prophet appeared again at the post office. He was in no mood to accept any of O'Hara's nasty mouth and sent him sprawling in the corner with the back of his giant hand.

"You make fun for me, no?" His voice was like thunder and his eyes swept the room.

"But I tell you something now you weel remembair! I perdick she will get cold and freeze an snow yet. And in June month I tell you too."

No one laughed - and it was just as well too, for the next day it turned bitter cold. A wild wind swept down from the northeast, blackening the flowers and the potatoes, shoving the people back inside their houses and the animals into the barns. And it got worse and worse. And it snowed and snowed and snowed through half of June.

But we got our Prophet back!

KING OF THE POACHERS

This story is about Laf Bodine, King of the Poachers, the most skillful violator Michigan's Upper Peninsula ever produced.

That honor really meant something special in our land of great granite hills, brimful lakes, deep snow and huge forests, a land where the game warden was generally regarded as a mortal enemy because he threatened the very survival of half the populace.

Most of the men of that time were violators of the game laws mainly because thay had to be in order to survive and partly because they enjoyed the sport of outwitting the conservation officers.

With the iron mines closed down and the logging activities uncertain after most of the giant white pine had been cut, there was little money for anything. Certainly there was none for "store meat" when the streams were full of trout, the lakes teeming with pike and the forests with rabbits, partridge and deer.

It's a bit hard to view the illicit activities of that time in proper perspective. The dynamiting of a beaver pond full of brook trout seems outrageous today, but back then those trout, carefully salted down in a barrel back in the woodshed, made the difference between eating or going hungry when March came. It's even difficult for me to remember the urgency connected with making sure the cellar shelves were crowded with jars of venison or canned wild berries - how important it was that there be a huge crock of sauerkraut, slabs of bacon and plenty of smoked or marinated fish on hand when the leaves turned gold and red.

Make it through the winter! Make it through the winter! That "command" was heard by all of us. Every autumn there was fear. Spring brought triumph, but with that triumph returned some of the urgency to start getting ready for another winter. The old bitter jest about, "Nine months of winter and three months of rough sledding," was not very funny to the people of the U.P. at the turn of the century.

There were years when every month brought a frosty night and I remember sleeping out once on the shore of Goose Lake in a heavy snow storm... That was on August, 3rd.

What I'm trying to say is that we needed all the fish and game we could get and we didn't particularly care how we got it.

The State Legislature, 400 miles away in Lansing, could pass all the game laws they wished, but we had to survive. They could send their game wardens north to catch us, if they could. Sometimes they did and sometimes they didn't, but all of us poached without the slightest sense of guilt.

Poor old Belanger was the laughing stock of the entire community because he always got caught. Whether haying or potato digging time, he always carried enough fine money in his pocket when he went shining deer because he had to stay out of jail long enough to get the crops in. Most of us were more adept.

The king of the poachers, though, was Laf Bodine. He was our hero, the most cunning and resourceful of all the violators in the Upper Peninsula. He'd made a career of it. Except for the month in the summer when he made pocket money guiding around a bunch of rich bastards from Chicago up at the Huron Mountain Club or when he was trapping, he probably did some violating every day of his life. His exploits were legend in our land. We admired him greatly. Moreover, Laf Bodine was sort of a Robin Hood. Any family that was having a rough go of it could expect to find a mess of fish or a couple of ducks or a haunch of venison on their back porch come daylight... especially if they were out of season!

They always knew who the giver was too, though Laf never mentioned it. You see, he always left his trademark - a slip of birch bark with a cedar twig stuck through it. Once or twice our family even found such an offering on the back porch. We found a big pike once and six blue winged teals another time, both gifts complete with birch bark and cedar. The reason my dad, the village doctor, was sure it was Laf was that when he saw him the next day, Laf had asked if he'd ever recieved payment for Mrs. So and So's medical bill. Dad grinned and said yes and Laf grinned too.

And there was the time when the Juntinen's horse got struck by lightning down in the Company Field. That horse had made a living for Toivo Juntinen and his eight young kids. Seven prime beaver hides, all skinned out and fleshed, enough to buy a new horse, the birch bark and cedar twig... All this they found in their outhouse the next morning.

When anyone got a present of illegal game or fish, they knew it was Laf's doing. Some winters they said he kept half the village alive. In return, for our people were very proud in their own way, Laf could always count on an occasional loaf of homemade bread, a dish of fresh butter or some Mason jars of canned blueberries to vary his meat diet. I remember once going out to Laf's cabin at Fish Lake with a friend of mine whose mother had knitted Laf some socks and mittens after she'd found a hind quarter of venison in their sauna building. The family hadn't eaten meat in over a month.

Laf's real name was Lafferty, named so as a slight gesture of affection - of revenge - by his mother Sarah, a full-blooded Menominee Indian, after Laf's probably father, a wild Irish mining engineer who had graced and raped our town for a few months in 1909. Perhaps that was why Laf had that shocking red head of hair that lit up the forest trails he strode. There were nine or ten other people in town with that same red hair and all were about the same age and fatherless, though that made little difference to anyone. You just had to be careful about whom you called a bastard! We took care of our own and a child was a child and always seemed to be welcome.

The original Laferty had been a giant of a man and smart, according to those who'd known him. He didn't drink or smoke, but he sure must have screwed everything in sight. He'd gotten himself fired after four months in town when the mining superintendent caught him with his seventeen year old daughter in the mining office. She too had a red headed baby, but had married a guy in Ishpeming and left town.

Anyway, Laf was a big man and as red headed as his father, but not so fond of women. He stayed pretty much clear of them. They say Nellie Bodner almost had her hooks in him once, but that broke up when Laf found out he'd have to buy a license. That went against his principles! A wife and kids would have just interfered with his life's chosen work anyway - poaching!

Much of what I write is hearsay because I only had one personal encounter with the king of the poachers and that was when I was only about nine years old.

It was on a Sunday afternoon in early spring. I'd hiked down the railroad tracks to see how far over the banks the Tioga River had flooded, thinking that I might try fishing there next day. There's a little feeder creek that parallels the tracks just above Red Bridge and below the tangle of an old beaver dam that plugged it, I saw the silver flash of fish.

"Ah," I'd said to myself. "Here's the time to learn how to tickle trout."

I'd heard how from my elders that, if you were very careful, you could put your hand in the pool, hold it there for a few minutes and then, if you rubbed your hand backward along their bodies, it would mesmerize them long enough to let you grab them by the tail and heave them up on the bank.

I sneaked down the bank very carefully, put my arm in up to my shoulder and almost yelped it was so cold, but I waited. A fish about a foot long did swim over my open palm several times, but whenever I tried to stroke it backwards, it fled. I remember almost weeping with cold and frustration when Laf was suddenly there beside me.

"No, boy," he'd said gruffly. "You're going about this all wrong. Here, let me show you."

He stripped to the waist revealing a massive chest covered, like his arms, with a mat of red hair. Then he lay down on the bank beside the little pool, watched and waited until one of the fish swam over his hand and stayed there, undulating in the current. I watched enthralled as Laf ever so slowly brought his palm upward and forward from tail to head, stroking the fish ever so lightly. Then, suddenly, up came his hand with the fish held firmly by the gills. It was a big sucker, not a trout, but I almost clapped.

"Well, that's the way to do it, boy," Laf said. "Hell, if you start at the head end like you were, you'll always scare 'em. You were also stroking too fast and too hard. Easy does it. Slow... Slow..."

Under his watchful eye and slightly bloodshot from a swallow of rotgut he'd offered, I managed to catch two more before my arms became almost paralyzed from the icewater. Laf noticed my uncontrollable shivering and built a little fire of dead willow twigs. I remember that it gave off plenty of heat and almost no smoke at all.

"Here, boy, arch your belly over the fire, like this, and you'll warm up fast, even your frozen arm. I'll go get an ironwood branch and show you a better way to catch suckers."

Laf disappeared as silently as he'd come, returning shortly with a black club, stripped of bark and all but one branch. Laf whittled the branch with a monstrous sheaf knife until it had a sharp point. The whole outfit looked like a four foot fish hook. Then he cut a notch just below the sharp point and hardened the sharp end of the stick in the glowing coals until it was charred black. Thrusting the contraption into the pool, he quickly snagged out another sucker, an even bigger one.

"Do it the same way," he said. "Come up from the back end, but jerk quick and hard!"

I soon caught on to the knack and had four of them on the bank before he took the stick away from me.

"How many you need?" he asked. "Every one you catch you got to take home and I figger you've got ten, maybe twelve pounds already. We don't waste 'em. We don't waste anything..."

He walked every foot of the three miles back to the depot to make sure I didn't throw any of those damned suckers away!

I thought my arms would fall off, but I learned a lesson; several of them. One was that Laf Bodine was quite a man.

Even the game wardens agreed to that.

We had a whole series of them, one after another, a new one almost every year. Some said the Conservation Department used our town as a training school with Laf acting at the teacher for new game wardens. He certainly bested them, ran rings around them and made them look foolish while the townspeople cheered.

For one thing, Laf's fame was such that any new game warden always concentrated on catching him, leaving the rest of our poachers free to fill their larders. It wasn't true that the State sent only new recruits to our town either. Some of their very best men came.

They watched Laf's cabin; tried to follow him in the woods, tried to anticipate what he'd do or where he'd strike next. Laf made monkeys out of them.

The best of it was that Laf had a left-handed way of bragging about his skill at outwitting game wardens and it kept us abreast of his exploits.

Almost every evening from eight to ten, he could be found by the pot-bellied stove in the depot waiting room or at a table in Higley's Saloon, telling tales about his Uncle Joe. There would always be a group of men around him, sharing the lore and lies of hunting, fishing and violating adventures, but when Laf spoke, after a couple of hookers of rotgut, they mainly listened, with awe and respect.

They knew, of course, that Laf never had an Uncle Joe and that Uncle Joe was him, but they learned a lot about the way to poach and not get caught, from the "master."

"My Uncle Joe," Laf would begin, "knew all there was to know about catching trout, but he used to claim he never et one in his life that was legal size. He liked the sweet little ones, five and six inchers, fried crisp in the pan till you could eat 'em bones and all.

"Oh, sometimes he might get him a glass jug, put some carbide in it, put a little hole in the cork and then wire it down good before heaving it into a beaver pond. Uncle Joe used to sometimes bring half a sackfull of trout and give 'em away to them that might be a-hungerin', people like Miz Olson up in Swedetown.

"You see, when the water leaks into the jug and the miner's carbide begins to fizz enough, boom goes the jug and there's your trout right on the surface. Just scoop 'em up. All sizes, but Uncle Joe he only kept the small ones. Said they were sweet as apple pie."

It didn't take much checking to find out that Mrs. Olson's kids had dined on trout the day before - and that they were small ones.

Whenever Laf voiced his opinion, not his Uncle Joe's, he was virtuous as hell.

"I don't approve of my Uncle Joe, that old reprobate," Laf would say. "The law may seem unreasonable, my friends, but them game wardens must do their duty, even if it means taking from the tables of the starving, the poor and the downhearted. Let me say it to you, my friends, any low down, no good son of a pup that'd violate them there laws should be hung from the nearest birch tree. That goes for my Uncle Joe too."

All the men in the saloon loved to listen as Laf supported the game wardens he bedeviled constantly.

In his depot and barroom tales of the exploits of Uncle Joe, Laf revealed many artisan secrets. He told how to use a set line in the spring when only a ring of water circled the shore, well before trout season opened; how to make a snare out of telephone wire for a deer runway; where to make a scaffold and how high up so the deer would walk right under it; when to dynamite pike during their spawning season; where to hide a deer you'd killed - in the outhouse, a dry well or under the hay in the barn.

I know one of his tales was true because I checked it out myself. There was always a deeryard over by Goose Lake when the snow got deep. Maybe a hundred or more deer wintered there and, as the game wardens found out, many of the families in our village relied on the area for their winter's meat supply.

It was hell trying to dodge the wardens once the snow came. You either went out hunting at the beginning of a blizzard, hoping the snow would cover your tracks, or you didn't go out at all. But, according to Laf, his Uncle Joe had solved the problem simply enough. He reversed the straps on his snowshoes and learned to walk with them that way.

Any game warden would think Uncle Joe was going south when, in fact, he was trudging along north.

I knew Laf and not his mythical Uncle Joe had actually done this because, one winter when I was snaring rabbits by Horseshoe Lake, I saw him going by down the trail and was amazed to see his tracks leading off the other way. The game wardens never caught on to the trick and you can bet none of the townspeople ever told him. You had to make it through the winter and it was good to know that Laf Bodine was not in jail!

Only once did Laf "almost" get caught.

Seventy year old Francois Perine, who had already reared one big brood of children, suddenly found himself saddled with another batch of kids when his youngest son and his wife had both died. All seven of their children had come back to town to live with the Perines in a cabin far too small for them. It was really rough going for the old man and Denise, his wife.

One December day, Laf came upon old Francois, lying in the snow completely bushed alongside a deer he'd dragged for half a mile through the snow. He still had to miles to go.

Laf knew the game warden was in the area, but he built a fire for the old man, boiled a can of water over it and inserted a sock with a handful of tea in the toe. When the water turned copper colored he gave some to Francois along with a lump of sugar. When he was sure the old man had revived, Laf tied the fore and hind legs of the deer together, flung it over his shoulder, and made his way to town with his backward snowshoes.

He dumped the deer off in Father Hassel, the Catholic Priest's carriage house so Francois could pick it up later. Then he went back to see how the old man was doing. There he found the game warden who promptly arrested Laf for removing the corpus delecti. The case never came to court though, because Father Hassel had found the deer and had hastily removed it... the corpus delecti.

But it was a close call.

Shortly after this incident, the State paid Laf Bodine the ultimate compliment. They formally offered him the job as game warden, $150 a month and a uniform.

All our townspeople waited anxiously while Laf made his decision. How would they dare violate if Laf were warden? How would they make it through the winter? Who would bring them meat when the children cried? They had no cause to worry. Laf didn't betray his people.

Laf never answered the game warden who offered him the job, but he acknowledged the compliment. He left a big chunk of venison, one trout and a partridge on the warden's doorstep - complete with a wisp of birch bark and a sprig of cedar.

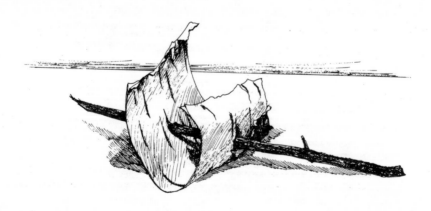

VALENTINE'S DAY

"Paul," my mother said, as dad finished his breakfast, "Don't run off to work like you usually do. Listen to me. Did you know that Aunt Lizzie is setting her cap for Bill Trager? It's outrageous! Why she must be, let's see, 54 - 55 and Bill can't be more than 33 or so. But there's no mistake. She's out to marry him. Poor Bill, such a nice man - weak maybe and he drinks too much sometimes, but a real nice man."

My father grinned. "You know, she just might pull it off at that. Bill can't say no to anything or anybody. Everyone takes advantage of him. But how do you know she's after Bill?"

My mother ticked the items off on her fingers:

"1. Aunt Lizzie has her hair 'frizzed' fresh on Tuesday and again on Thursday, instead of only on Saturday, when she used to curl it for church.

"2. She bought raisins, brown sugar, some yeast and some flour at the store and she never had before. Going to bait Bill with cookies and home-made bread.

"3. Mrs. Casey saw Aunt Lizzie stop Bill Tuesday morning and bring him into her house - back door - and when Mrs. Casey just happened to take the opportunity to return the cup of sugar she'd borrowed, Aunt Lizzie was plying Bill with cookies and flirting outrageously, primping and being coy, as they had coffee together, tete-a-tete.

"God!" growled my father. "Everybody knows everything that happens in this town. Mrs. Casey borrows sugar from all her neighbors just so she can horn in any time she wants. Has she borrowed any from you, Edith?"

My mother made a little face and nodded.

"OK, buy her a sack so she won't find out when I cut my toenails!"

"But how about Bill? Is he falling for the snare? I always thought he was kind of sweet on Annie, the postmistress."

"Oh, that was a long time ago," replied my mother. "I still think it would have been a good match, but they're both too sweet and kinda shy. Neither would take the first step.

No, Aunt Lizzie sure knows how to handle a man like that. Lead him by the nose right up to the church door... Like she did her other two husbands," continued mother.

"Yeah, and killed them both," said dad. "Nagged them to death! Any man can't tell a woman to shut up deserves his fate. Well, anyway, there goes Bill Trager. Old Aunt Lizzie's got him!"

I was very upset. I bent lower over my Cream of Wheat.

Annie and Bill were special people in my life and Aunt Lizzie sure wasn't. I couldn't stand that old hag, the old simpering fake. I couldn't bear her bossiness at Sunday School or the horrible way she whined those high notes off key on the hymns. A nasty woman. She mustn't trap poor Bill into marrying her. If she did, he'd have to leave the little 40-acre homestead that he'd hewn out of the forest down by the lake and go live with her and those pictures of her dead husbands that hung in her parlor by the horsehair sofa. Those pictures had the pupils of the eyes dead-center so they seemed to follow you wherever you went in the room.

And Bill wouldn't be able to have any time for a small boy like me to help him know how to hitch up a horse - or to plow - or to whittle - or to listen to the wonderful tales of his Navy experiences... Like the time he found "Waterloo, Iowa" tatooed on the hind end of a girl in Marseilles.

Hell, Bill Trager would die, being married to someone like Aunt Lizzie. She'd make him dress up and shave every day like Silly Billy, the village idiot. If he married her, Bill wouldn't be able to keep his chickens and pig or his old horse that he treated to a big handful of oats every Fourth of July, saying, "Eat till ye bust!"

And I liked Bill's log cabin. It was halfway to the lake, a good place to stop, all full of junk - padlocks, magnets, tools and bits of old harness. I dropped in often in the summer on my way for a swim, but even in the winter I would make my way down to his homestead for a pleasant afternoon. Bill seemed to like me. I certainly liked him.

I also liked Annie, the postmistress. You see, I helped deliver the mail.

Old Man Marteau who was responsible for bringing up the mail from the depot by sleigh in the winter and buckboard in the summer, lived right behind our house. Once he'd operated a livery stable, a flourishing one, but he was down to just a couple of horses and rigs by the time I got to know him. Nevertheless, every day -- rain, snow or shine -- he met the Duluth, South Shore and Atlantic (trainmen called it the DSS&A, "Damned Small Salary and Abuse"), every morning and evening, hauling the mail bags to the downtown post office and then to the uptown post office where Annie presided.

Old Man Marteau had arthritis pretty bad.

I remember my father calling me one hot summer's day to come see the old man buried to his neck in a manure pile and holding a little pink umbrella over him to fend off the sun.

"A good treatment," said my father. "Moist warm heat and pressure. My pharmacopeia has nothing better."

Anyway, Old Man Marteau was glad enough in his surly way, to have me help him with his chores. I'd ride down to the station with him, get the mail bags when they were thrown down from the mail car, load them in the rig and carry them into the two post offices. I was also elected to use the long buggy whip to keep the other kids from hitching rides with their sleds and wagons.

The mail bags usually weren't too heavy for me except at Christmas and seed catalogue time, and I would bring them into the inner sanctum sanctorum of Annie's post office with real pride, because there was a sign on the door that said: "Private Property of the United States Government. Unauthorized Personnel Forbidden to Enter."

Once inside and behind the wall of pigeon holes and lock boxes, Annie would let me unlock the mail bags and do some of the preliminary sorting. It sure made me feel important.

Annie was a rather plain woman, about 30, but she had a sweet smile and a very soft voice. I liked her. Everybody liked her, though some suspected that she steamed open letters and read their mail. She certainly knew a lot about all the people in town.

Anyway, I decided to pay Bill Trager a visit one afternoon. He was sharpening a scythe with a long hone. It seemed a bit odd since it was only the first week of February with drifts higher than a man's head everywhere. I'd had a hard time getting down to Bill's place even with the trail well broken.

I found Bill morose and without any good stories. He just kept sharpening that scythe, zing - zing, spitting on the hone to make it work better.

Being only eleven years old, I just couldn't keep still any longer.

"Bill," I said, "They're saying old Aunt Lizzie is going to marry you. You aren't going to let her do that, are you?"

Bill put down his scythe and lit his pipe.

" Well," he said, "She's got me scared, I'll admit. Everytime I go past her house on my way for the mail, it's 'Mister Trager, would you kindly fix this poor widow's doorknob - or help move her settee' or she's out shoveling snow and asks for just a little help. And then she feeds me good vittles - Damned good vittles. A lot better than my bacon and beans and coffee-pail-bread. Of course, she's old enough to be my mother, but what's wrong with having a mother? Ah, that's crazy talk. Enough."

He fell silent and I eventually left, really worried. But what could one small boy do?

I decided to try to do something, nevertheless.

I went down to Flinn's store and bought a bunch of store valentines. I had to rob my businessman bank, the one where you put a coin in the little seated man's hand and he'd drop it into his vest pocket. Anyway, I bought seven valentines, addressed three of them to Annie and three to Bill and signed their names appropriately. I forget now what I wrote on the lacy things all full of hearts and flowers, but it was something like, "I've kept loving you all these years," for the first card, then I progressed to, "I hunger for you, my dear" and "I'll be at the post office tonight at eight-thirty. Please come, my true love."

It was hard for an eleven-year-old to write that doggone mushy stuff, but I did and I wrote the same on each pair of valentines, one for Annie and one for Bill. I felt a little guilty signing their names like that, but I had to do something to stop Aunt Lizzie.

Then, each night after dark, I'd walk down to the post office and drop the letters with the valentines in them into the slot of the locked door. I sure worried hard about the whole business.

Finally, about a week after Valentine's Day had come and gone, I went back to delivering the mail bags again. I don't really know what happened, but Annie was looking almost pretty and she kissed me. Blaugh! Wet lips! I wiped them off as she turned to the teakettle on the potbellied stove and held up the envelope against it impishly.

"You're a good boy and you had a marvelous idea and it worked!" Annie flushed. "But it was the seventh valentine that helped most of all!" she said.

I knew what she meant. It was the one I'd bought for Aunt Lizzie and signed Bill Trager's name to. Lord, it was a horrible one, an old fashioned comic valentine, featuring an ugly old woman with warts and wens, and bearing a verse inscribed with a blackened heart:

Lizzie,

"Roses are red and violets are blue,
But How in the hell could anyone love you."

Bill Trager

96

GRAMPA

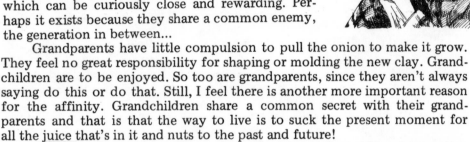

This is a story about the biggest trout ever taken from the Tioga River. You may not particularly like trout or stories about them, but you sure would have liked my Grampa Gage, and I can't tell about the one without telling about the other.

There is a special sort of relationship that exists between grandparents and grandchildren which can be curiously close and rewarding. Perhaps it exists because they share a common enemy, the generation in between...

Grandparents have little compulsion to pull the onion to make it grow. They feel no great responsibility for shaping or molding the new clay. Grandchildren are to be enjoyed. So too are grandparents, since they aren't always saying do this or do that. Still, I feel there is another more important reason for the affinity. Grandchildren share a common secret with their grandparents and that is that the way to live is to suck the present moment for all the juice that's in it and nuts to the past and future!

Anyway, Grampa and Grandma Gage came to live with us from spring to autumn during the two years when I was nine and ten. They were two of the most delightful years of my life, not because of Grandma (she was a nasty, razor-tongued old she-devil), but because Grampa Gage was mine, all mine. He was my 74 year-old playmate, mentor, model and constant companion. A boy of 9 or 10 has a deep hunger for identification and association with a man, a hunger that my own father had neither the time nor the inclination to satisfy. I was lucky, very lucky to have my Grampa Gage.

He was a short man, but very wiry and tough. He had been a farmer, lumberjack, teamster, grocer, banker and bankrupt, in that order. He'd gone bankrupt because his best friend, the cashier at the bank, had absconded to South America with most of the liquid assets. All that Grampa had left after the inevitable run on the bank were his sense of humor and his dignity. It was a bit surprising that he had managed to retain either because Grandma Gage's tongue never let him forget the bank failure, even though she had lots of money and stocks of her own and the house in her name. Perhaps it was because she felt compelled to constantly humiliate Grampa in public that he found the relief and escape he needed in our relationship, but I don't believe it. Grampa Gage just liked being with me.

Each day began at 5:30 with Grampa shaving in the bathroom beside my bedroom. He'd be lathering his face (and often a bit of mine), with copious suds, twisting it into a hundred contortions - all funny ones - as he stroked at it with the gleaming straight razor. Next, he'd comb the gray mustache that always had a smile flickering beneath it and he'd turn to me.

"Well, Mr. McGillicuddy, shall we do our exercises?"

He had a new name for me every day and he used that name all day except when other people were around. Then he just called me "Boy."

So we'd do our exercises, then go down to the kitchen, make a pot of coffee and share some toast and conversation before any of the rest of the family woke up. Grampa Gage never talked down to me the way most grown-ups did.

"Mr. McGillicuddy," he would say, "I would appreciate your opinion, sir, on the prospects for another nice day" or "Mr. Gallupus, what, sir, is the a-gend-a for our morning adventure?"

His blue eyes always twinkled, but his face and manner were completely serious. Whatever I gave would be considered gravely.

If, for example, I would say that we might start building a shack hide-away down in the grove behind the chicken coop, Grampa Gage would give it some long, silent thought, pursing his lips, furrowing his brow and nodding before replying, "Well, Mr. Anderanderanderson, I agree. Let us indeed erect a Taj Mahal this fine day. Where, sir, do you think we might find the necessary and appropriate e-quip-ment, sir? A hammer perhaps?"

Grampa used lots of big words which he never explained unless I asked, but he would sound them out now and then.

Some mornings when it became time to decide what to do, Grampa would say, "Enjoy. Just enjoy!"

Some days all we would do would be to collect different shades of green, or taste plants like soursap, nettles and Indian tobacco, or just feel rocks. Other days we would hunt holes and hide treasures in them for another day; a sugar lump, a piece of gum, or a note to Mother Earth.

Perhaps the most important thing I learned from Grampa was to have a gay spirit and not to be afraid of fantasy or afraid to do or say nutty things.

For one thing, Grampa was always rhyming.

He'd point to a sapling and say, "I'd like to be that birch. Wouldn't have to go to church."

But most of the time he made Grampa Goosers, as he called them.

"Fiddle Dee Dee, Fiddle Dee Dee, Grandma sat down on a bumblebee. The bee stung her twice. Now wasn't that nice? And her bottom's as red as can be. Tee Hee! Her bottom's as red as can be."

Or he'd suddenly ask me if I'd ever seen a frog cry and proceed to tell me a long tale about a monster frog he once saw rocking back and forth on its haunches just dripping with tears and moaning, "Why am I the only frog in the world who doesn't know how to jump?"

Well, Grampa said he felt really sorry for the varmint, especially when the other frogs in the swamp, not half his size, were teasing him and calling him "Kindergarten baby, slopped in the gravy."

So Grampa said he got down beside the frog, told him how to jump and showed him how.

"And then, Boy, you know what I did? I took out this here pencil while he was thinking over what I'd told him and I give that old frog the goosiest goose up the hind end you ever did see. An' he took off like a pro-jeck-tile, he did, right up straight in the air, and lit on a tree branch. I had a devil of a time getting him down and told him to take it easier next time, but he didn't. Just kept jumpin' and jumpin' and jumpin', higher and higher every time, and one moonlit night he scrunched down and took off and nobody ever saw him again. Some say there's a man in the moon you can see if you look right close, but 'pears to me it looks more like that there frog. I'd 'preciate knowing what you see, Mr. O'Flaherty, next time you get the chance."

Grampa always told the best stories after he'd had a snort or two from the little black bottle in his hip pocket. He never let me taste it though.

"Save something for your old age, Mr. O'Flaherty. Save something for your old age," he'd say.

Sometimes I just had to ask him if his stories were true.

Like the time he told me about General Gage, who during the Revolutionary War, while in command of the British troops after they captured Boston, had seduced a fair young American maiden under a rose bush.

"And from that issue, Mr. O'Toole, all the Gages have come, including you, Mr. O'Toole. Though you bear not the name, yet that noble blood runs in your veins, as you shall know one day when with girl under a rose, Mr. O'Toole."

Grampa looked at me hard. "And what's more, Boy, I put upon you a command. You are not to di-vulge, which is to say, tell any female relative of mine what I have imparted to you this day. I mean both Grandma Gage and her daughter, your mother, or your own daughter or her daughters, but you shall tell your son and your son's son this thing."

I was very impressed, especially when he insisted that I swear to do his bidding by "the immortal grace of the daisies" in which we were sitting at the time, but I still couldn't help asking if it was really true.

"Should it be true?" roared Grampa. "Should it be true?"

His question has beset me all the rest of my life.

Wild and wonderful as our conversations were, there were times when our actions were just as zany.

Like the time we had been on safari, hunting lions in deepest Africa, down in the meadow. Not real lions, ant lions, those curious beetles that make a funnel in the sand to trap any unwary insect that ventures along its slope.

Grampa would say a magic word like "Oogalalamo!," tickle the side of the funnel with a straw and out of the hole would come the ant lion, clicking its jaws. Then we'd run like hell and Grampa would have to take a swig or two from his black bottle to "re-gain" his courage.

"Out of the jaws of death, it's hard to catch your breath," he'd say.

I think that was the time, too, that he taught me 'The Dance of the Wild Cucumber.' I can still see Grampa doing it, crossing his arms in the air and chanting the refrain ecstatically, "O Tweedle Dee and Tweedle Dum, All Hail Immortal Nose and Thumb" - always with the appropriate gesture on the final word. I got pretty good at it finally.

It was always difficult for me to understand or accept the drastic shift in role that took place in Grampa Gage's behavior when he returned to the house. As soon as he entered the door, he suddenly became another person; quiet, dignified and solemn. No more jokes. No wild flights of fancy. He was just very polite and reserved.

What was worse, he became Grandma's slave and whipping boy.

"Arzeeeee!" she would screech (his name was Arza), "Fetch me my scissors. Fetch me this. Fetch me that. Quick now, stonefoot, stonehead! Why did I ever marry a slug like you, Arzeeeee? I said fetch my scissors."

"I'm coming, Nettie. I'm coming. I've found your scissors."

Grampa wouldn't hurry, but he always did her bidding. And then she lashed at him with all the caustic invective she could muster while he just stood there calmly and waited for her to stop. She'd humiliate him so much that I wanted to throw the coal scuttle at her sometimes. Grandma Gage was not a nice person and she caused quite a strain in our household. Just to give one minor example of her irritating ways - At the table she would never ask politely for something she wanted like Grampa always did. Instead, she'd snarl, "Have you got a mortgage on that butter?"

She was a female hellion and how Grampa took it and bore her clacking all those years was a mystery.

I explored the matter with him once and he told me the story of Socrates and his shrewish wife, Xantippe. How once the philosopher had come home late from drinking with the boys to find the door locked. At his knock, Xantippe poked her head out the window above and gave him blue fits, getting angrier and angrier with every nasty word, finally to a point where she emptied the chamber pot over his head. Grampa paused and relit his pipe.

"And then, Mr. O'Hallahan, Socrates proved, sir, that he was indeed a true philosopher. He wiped his brow and said, 'After the thunder comes the rain.' I, Mr. O'Hallahan, am not a philosopher, but even I know that even the widest river runs somewhere safe to sea."

I had another glimpse that shed some light on their curious relationship. It came right after I'd done something very bad. I don't remember what it was, but it was bad because even Grampa was upset with me.

True to character, however, he never mentioned it directly, but while walking down the back road to the lake, he began talking about the trees and bushes as though they were people.

"Now that lovely birch sapling there, that's your mother. And that fine spruce is your father. A bit hard to climb up on, and scratchy, but a good stout tree. Now look at this young maple seedling, Boy. It's beginning to grow crooked, growing all wrong. Let's straighten it up, Boy."

I understood immediately that I was the young maple and I began to cry. Grampa comforted me, and to distract me from my woe, pointed out a large hawthorne full of thorns and red haw berries. I put one of the haws in my mouth and began to nibble at it.

"Cannibal, Cannibal!" Grampa hollered. "Stop eating Grandmaw."

I burst into laughter, thinking how thorny she was, but then Grampa interrupted in a wistful, far away voice, "But, ah, that hawthorne was lovely in the spring, Boy."

I've probably told you too much about my Grampa, but you still can't really know what he was like unless I tell you about that big trout.

At that time, no one in the Upper Peninsula ever fished for anything but northern pike and trout. We preferred the latter.

My father, who lived to be 94, attributed his long life to the fact that the only days that counted were those on which he didn't go trout fishing! He had the fever - but he was a meat fisherman, counting a trip successful only when he returned with his basket full to the brim.

Grampa was different. He was a fly fisherman and perfectly content to bring back just a fish or two, usually those that had been injured in the battle with the hook and line. The rest he returned to the water with a long and proper admonition about things not being what they seem.

One of the aches I remember from childhood was that my dad wouldn't ever take me fishing with him. When he did manage to steal a few hours from his work, he preferred to fish with his cronies, wading up to his armpits in the big river, dunking his worms and always after as many trout as he could get. He used to twit Grampa about fly fishing, telling him that all he'd ever get on flies were the baby ones, that any decent trout wanted the biggest night crawler that could be found.

That didn't bother Grampa any and he was bound that I would learn to fly fish. So for about a month we'd walk down Company Field Hill and across the swamp to Beaver Dam Creek so I could practice with his flyrod. It was hard to get the knack of it until Grampa had me practice putting a green apple on a stick and flinging it off suddenly. After that it was easy. When I even caught a small trout or two from the pond, Grampa said I was ready for a real fishing ex-ped-ition.

And so, one fine summer afternoon, there we were in the buckboard, riding up the logging trail that runs alongside the Tioga, the old horse stepping lively under the slap of the reins. We even had a little adventure when old Billy suddenly began to snort and rear and refused to take another step.

"Now what the tarnation has got into him?" asked Grampa. Then he sniffed. "Oh, oh. Smell it, Boy? Bear smell. One must have crossed here short time ago."

Grampa got off and led Billy past the place and I got a whiff of it, rank and strong.

There wasn't any more trouble, but I was a bit scared going down the steep incline of Campbell's hill. I remember the song the old loggers had about it.

"Going up Campbell's hill, coming down,
"Going up Campbell's hill, coming down,
"With the horse standing still and the wheels going round
"Going up Campbell's hill, coming down."

It was steep, but Grampa sure knew how to handle a horse.

When Grampa finally stopped and unharnessed Billy to feed him some oats and a chunk of hay from the back of the wagon, I was almost jumping with excitement. We gathered our gear and made our way down a narrow trail that angled kitty-corner along the bluff to the river bottom and the lovely pool below the broken old bridge. It was a long pool bordered by reddish gravel from the overhanging cliff. There was plenty of room for the back cast.

Grampa was in no hurry as he put the gut leader to soak in a little pool beside the log where he sat. He even refilled his pipe before he assembled his bamboo flyrod.

"Now, Boy," he said observing my impatience, "let's just wait a mite till you calm down or you'll forget everything you've learned. Where would you say, sir, that you would be a-lying were you a fat, hungry trout?"

I pointed to a foam circled eddy at the head of the pool.

"Mebbe so, mebbe so," replied Grampa, "but let's save that for later and begin casting down at the tail of the run. You'll often find a lazy one in such a place just a-waiting for you. Mind though, that if one takes your fly, you keep him out of those old beaver cuttings."

Then he took a leather covered fly box out of his inside coat pocket and asked me to pick out two of the wet flies, one for the dropper and one for the end of the leader. I selected the brightest ones, a red and white Parmachene Belle, and the blue and white Silver Doctor. Grampa raised his bushy eyebrows questioningly, but tied them on.

"Whose turn first?" he asked as we finally rose from the log.

It was hard, but I managed to say that I thought it ought to he his turn first so he could show me how to do it, that I might throw a sloppy line and spoil it for him. Grampa gave the decision some thought then said no, he'd take his turn later.

"Now Boy," he admonished, "I'm going to say only three things and, may God help me, not a word more. Cast a little bit upstream as slow and easy as you can. Take up the slack as it drifts down so you'll have a tight line. Any trout will hook hisself then. And DON'T HORSE 'EM IN or I'll beat your damned tail off."

He almost scared me, he sounded so ferocious.

Well, I didn't do too badly the first two casts. Caught a trout on each of them. Not very big ones, maybe ten inchers, but I switched hands and played them off the reel just like Grampa had shown me until I had them near the shore. Then I swung them back on the gravel for him to take off. I had just begun the backcast for the third try when I remembered about taking turns and I made a mess of it while I was telling Grampa I'd forgotten and was sorry. You just can't talk and cast a fly at the same time. As I handed him the rod, he told me we'd have to wait a bit because the splash of the rod tip along with the tangled line had surely put the trout down.

"Let's just con-tem-plate and enjoy," he urged as he lit his pipe and puffed for the longest time, sending pale blue rings of smoke drifting past me. I cleaned my two beautifully speckled trout and put them in the basket.

"Is it time for me to try again, Grampa? It must be an hour."

He was amused at my impatience and showed me on his gold watch that only 13 minutes had gone by.

"Well," he said, "I see the fever's on you, Boy, so why don't you take the rod up to the head of the pool and cast there at the base of that riffle while we're waiting for these to calm down. But first, here's one for the gentleman!" and Grampa pulled out the black bottle from his hip pocket, took a hefty gulp, then dipped both flies in the liquor. "That's for luck. Go catch us a sloib, as the Finns would say."

Grampa's nose was hovering over the bottle again so I went along the gravel upstream about a hundred feet, made a couple of good back casts and let the line go out. A perfect cast for once! The flies lit on the water like eiderdown and had barely sunk beneath the surface when WHAM! The rod was almost pulled out of my hand and the tip bent under the water as the reel whirred under my hand. Something terribly heavy tore my line down- stream toward Grampa - then over across to the other bank, then back almost to my feet, then up into the riffle where I saw it for the first time. A monster fish! I wish I could remember what actually happened, but I couldn't then and I can't now. All I recall is Grampa running up and down the gravel, hollering and praying.

102

"Keep the rod up! Oh, dear Lord, turn him, turn him, quick, before he gets in that snag! Boy! Let him have it! Let him have it! Crank, crank, crank! Take up the slack! Take up the slack! Tight line, Boy! Tight line! Let him wear himself out. Lord. oh Lord, don't let him get off!"

I know I did everything wrong. I even slipped on a rock once and sat down hard with my butt in the water, but I kept the rod high even then. I don't know how long the battle lasted - a minor eternity - but the big trout finally began to tire and I started to move him in closer to the sandbar where I was standing, knee-deep in the stream.

Grampa was still hollering at me.

"Now back up, Boy! Back up slowly! He's coming in. Oh Lord, don't let him get away now! Back way up on the bank, Boy. No, no, keep the rod high. Easy now..."

Grampa waded in behind the fish, and with him splashing behind and me pulling, it thrashed and wiggled and slid right up on dry land. Grampa leaped upon it, pinning it safely to the gravel while I put the rod down and came shakily over to see what I'd caught.

"Never was such a trout. Never!" yelped Grampa, panting as he unhooked the fly.

"Look, it won't possibly fit in the basket. Good thing we brought the wagon! Here, Boy, here's your fish. Put him way up there in the shade.

It was even hard for me to lift it, it was so heavy. I had to use both hands. Grampa sat down on the log, his hands trembling. He could hardly get the little black bottle to his mouth.

"C'mon here, Boy! This calls for a cel-e-bration."

He rummaged in a pocket and brought out a collapsable tin cup which he filled with river water. Then he poured a little liquor in from the black bottle.

"A toast to the King of the River!" he said. "Drink it down, King! Drink it down!"

It tasted like river water and I spit it out as I went back to admire the big fish and allow Grampa to get over the shakes.

103

He must have gotten over them for he suddenly gave a great yell and there he was, doing the 'Dance of the Wild Cucumber' all the way up to the bridge and back.

"You're turn Grampa, your turn." I motioned to the rod.

"Dunno if I have the strength to hold it," he replied. "But I'll try her a couple of times and then we'll go home and show your folks what the King of the River has caught. Don't worry about the trout. He's safe. I tunked him over the head with a rock and he won't get away. You'd better go up to the rig and put a lot of ferns under the seat so he'll keep fresh and won't lose color on the way home."

Up on the hill beside the road I found enough ferns for several armsful, but between carries I went partway down the trail to see how Grampa was doing.

Hey, he had a fish on too. And a big one. Another monster. Bigger than mine? Yes, it was! I had an empty sinking feeling in my stomach... But why was Grampa doing everything wrong?

He was jerking the line, horsing the fish, trying to lead it into the snag! And why was he fumbling for something in his pocket?

A moment later he slid the great trout up on the bank, cut the leader right at the fly and gently shoved the fish back into the water with his foot.

Carrying my trout, he met me coming down the trail. Grampa pointed to the broken leader before I could say anything.

"Let's call it a day, Boy. Snapped off my leader on a snag and lost the flies. Let's go home."

It was a long ride home behind the old horse clomping down the road, but it was worth it when dad, mother and Grandma Gage came out to the barnyard to see how we'd done.

"How many you get?" asked dad.

"Only three," I answered.

"But there's only two here in the basket," he said, peering into it.

Then I showed him what was in the ferns under the seat.

"Well, I'll be damned. Never saw such a trout. I'll be damned. Go four pounds. On a fly too? Impossible!"

"And how about you, Arzee?" demanded Grandma. "How about you?"

"Aw, I got skunked," said Grampa happily.

That's the kind of man he was.

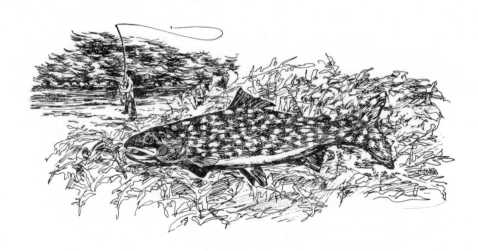

OLD BLUE BALLS

A violent war between the 'Uptowners and the Downtowners' had been waged sporadically for many years in the little village where I was born and spent my childhood.

The town had two centers, each with a store and tiny post office. One was in the valley, the other at the crest of the hill. A straggle of houses lined the one street that joined them.

The railroad station and a community of French Canadians and a few half-breed Indians were situated in the valley. On top of the hill lived the Finns, a few Swedes, three or four Cornish ex-miners who hadn't left when the iron mine closed, and the rest of us. The school with its playground battlefield divided the two areas.

It was Catholics versus Protestants in a neighborhood war of the roses - or bloody noses. You had to fight to survive. I had more black eyes and puffed lips in my day than any prize fighter, but so did all the rest of the kids.

Every school day produced a few fights, individual or gang. The chip on the shoulder was reality.

"I kin lick you!"

"Let's go down and get the Frogs!"

"Pass the word. The Suomalinas (Finns) are coming. Get your clubs."

There were no Marquis of Queensbury rules - only one: No fair kicking in the crotch! We fought until they ran or until we ran, bloody from the field.

The mayhem peaked twice each year: in the fall when the first snow packed well enough to make iceballs and in late spring when the snow was almost gone and we could take off the itching underwear - usually May. Hell, in the spring you just had to do something outrageous. We fought. It wasn't enough to just piss in some other kid's maple sap buckets. You had to raise real hell. Like young bucks, we had to lock horns and charge. Spring always had the best - or worst - battles royal. Like the sap, blood had to flow. It was tradition!

Oddly enough, now 50 years later, the fighting has stopped. The Finns and the French have intermarried. The kids nowadays make love and play organized baseball. The towns have come together, become one, are homogenized and pasteurized. The old tradition of battle is ended. This is the tale of how that war finally stopped and how peace came to the village at last. It's the tale of the big shit fight and how we got the best of Old Blue Balls, the school superintendent.

To understand, you would have had to know Old Blue Balls Donegal. His 'real name' was Mister Donegal or Old Man Donegal, but everyone called him "Sininen Pollu," a Finnish phrase meaning dark blue testicles, and we used the English translation...Behind his back!

To his face it was always, "Yes, Mr. Donegal. No, Mr. Donegal."

Old Blue Balls was tough. In his late fifties when I knew him, he was in perfect physical condition with a wrestler's torso. He was short and looked thin, but oh, was he in shape.

When he looked at you hard with his electric blue eyes, the impact was almost that of a physical blow. He had gray bushy eyebrows and two deeply engraved furrows on each side of a widely slit mouth which eventually joined a jutting lower jaw. There was a spring to his walk and he always appeared half ready to pounce, probably because he kept his great clubs of fists slightly in front of his thighs and didn't alternate his arms like most people do when they walk. Donegal looked tough and he was. In that rough land and time he had to be.

The story of how he was hired and how he took charge illustrates the point.

Our school had been in some trouble because a minor depression had halted most of the logging operations for a year or two. Ordinarily, when a boy got big enough to lick the teacher or the superintendent, he was big enough to start cutting pulp. Few ever finished high school, but since there wasn't any work in the bush, the big boys stayed in school and made life miserable for all of us and especially for the teachers. The matter came to a head on opening day of the fall semester when a new superintendent and two or three new teachers arrived. The old ones had quit to nurse their bruises.

Among the new teachers was a Miss Crough who looked like an old black broom. The first morning session went well enough, but when the teachers came back to school after lunch, they had to walk the gauntlet of boys sitting on the fence that lined the schoolyard. All of them were being ominously quiet and polite - until Miss Crough came along. Then every boy on the fence cawed like a crow. They cawed in time to her steps. When she hurried, they cawed faster; when she lagged, they slowed down. She became angry and slapped one of the smaller boys, a mistake, for she then found herself leading a procession of cawing boys up the board sidewalk and into the building. And that wasn't the end of it. Caws were heard all over the school intermittently, for the rest of the day. Even in kindergarten! The superintendent called the constable who came and laughed and left. At seven-thirty that night, when Miss Crough, the other new teachers and the new superintendent boarded the train for Green Bay and Chicago, the school board met in emergency session to make plans for their replacement.

Anyway, that's how we wound up with Old Man Donegal, an honors graduate from the University of Chicago who loved to fish and hunt and who was so broke when he arrived that he had to borrow three dollars for food.

He sized up the situation instantly and made his presence felt by calling each and every pupil into his office. He began with the biggest ones. These he thrashed thoroughly, one after another, using his fists on the older tougher kids, a razor strop on the middle sized, a ruler for the smaller children and a gentle swat with the flat of his hand for the tiniest ones. Only the last ones got an accompanying grin.

The rest heard the same roar:

"Now take this and this and this! And let me tell you something. If I ever hear of you making any trouble around this school for anyone or if I catch you at it, I'll tan the tarnation hide right off you!"

Donegal meant it too. He demonstrated year after year. He ran a tight ship, terrorizing pupils and teachers alike. He'd often invade a classroom, watch what was going on for a moment and then take over the teaching himself if he didn't like what he saw. Loitering in the halls was even dangerous. He'd appear unexpectedly and accost you with questions:

"How much is eighty-seven times forty-three?

"What's the capital of Constantinople?

"Who was Daniel Boone?"

If you couldn't answer, you had to find out pronto and report in his office on the third floor of the three story frame building that was our schoolhouse. It was so old it swayed in the wind gusts. Anyway, no one ever entered that horror sanctum on the third floor without trembling, guilty or not.

Old Man Donegal was also very patriotic. All of us had to know every word of the Star Spangled Banner by heart and be prepared to sing it anywhere, on command. I recall one time during World War I, when the classroom door suddenly burst open and Mr. Donegal poked his head in to yell, "Forty Thousand Germans Killed. Hooray, Hooray, Hooray!"

When we failed to join in on the last hurrah, he entered and had us yell it for fifteen minutes.

He was also his own truant officer, not loathe to invade a home and drag a crying youngster out from under the bed. He always knew where we'd sneak off to go fishing or swimming and often as not he'd get to Fish Lake and be hiding in the bushes at Big Rock before we got there. He'd always wait though, until we'd taken off our clothes, before jumping out and whaling us. He was omniscient, omnipresent and omnipotent. We feared and hated Old Man Donegal intensely, but we sure respected him. He was always one move ahead and he always got the best of us -

Except once.

I was in the eighth grade then.

The year before, someone or something, maybe lightening, had burned down the old wooden school building and some of our classes were being held in my father's hospital across the street. That was where Donegal had his office.

Behind the hospital were two outhouses, each divided into two compartments with a hole in each. One of our favorite tricks was waiting for some unsuspecting soul to sit down to do his duty and inserting a switch under the hole in the other compartment and banging the kid's ass. I remember such experiences vividly.

Well, one day at recess, Old Man Donegal entered one of the outhouse doors and some kid came up with the ingenious idea of telling Sulu Lahti, who'd just come out, that Emil, his worst enemy, was taking a crap - and here's a good club, Sulu.

Sulu fell for it and whopped Old Blue Balls' ass a good one.

When his terrible roar shattered the silence, we all fled... All except Sulu.

Old Man Donegal charged out of the outhouse, holding his pants up with one hand and reaching for Sulu with the other. Oh, was he mad! And he got madder, trying to hold, hit and keep his pants up all at the same time.

Under the stress, Sulu's command of the English language failed him:

"Exercise me, Mr. Donegal. Exercise me!" (He'd meant "excuse me").

The superintendent's bellow echoed over the hills:

"I'LL EXERCISE YOU ALL RIGHT! I'LL EXERCISE YOU LIKE YOU'VE NEVER BEEN EXERCISED BEFORE!"

Wow! What a walloping! Sulu wasn't able to sit down for a week, but he was a hero to all of us, Uptowners and Downtowners alike. He was the only one in the world who had ever gotten even with Old Blue Balls Donegal, the only one who had given him a good crack on the ass - Sulu, the avenger.

So now to the end of the hill war. The battle that was to end all battles took place at dusk one day in late May, just before school let out for the year. It had been a long bitter winter and the harsh discipline of the class-room was becoming unbearable. Individual fights and group skirmishes were increasing. Without snow, we had turned to fists and even stones. Blood really flowed. One boy was seriously injured when he got hit in the head with a chunk of iron ore. Old Man Donegal decided to step in right then. He visited every classroom and delivered the same message. Anyone who threw a stone, a big one or a small one, in the schoolyard or elsewhere, and hit another child with it would be dealt with severely.

"I'll scrape every bit of skin from his hide!" was the way he'd put it.

That put sort of a crimp in our plans and a damper on our anticipations. Plans had already been made for that evening's mayhem with challenges made and accepted. But then some kid came up with a bright idea.

"OK," he said. "No stones. Horse turds. They're almost as hard as stones anyway after a day or two in the sun."

Agreed.

We went ahead with our preparations.

God, but we were ingenious! Warfare was the mother of invention! There was always a way to get around any rule!

You have to remember that this was in the day before automobiles. There were only two in town then and the farmers were still bringing their teams up to smell my dad's Ford so they wouldn't bolt and run away when they met him on the road.

There were lots of horses in town and lots of cows. They roamed at will. Every night, while I lay abed, I could hear the clomp-clomp of some old nag making its way up the pine-board sidewalk that ran along one side of the street across from the house. And there was always the tinkle of cowbells.

The cows and the horses both preferred the sidewalk to the street for some reason - perhaps because they liked the sound of their reverberating hoofs. Anyway, I could never figure out why they always shit more on the way up the hill than on the way down, but they did. Maybe it was the extra effort. Anyway, they seemed to produce more manure on the steepest part of the grade, right in front of Old Man Donegal's house, opposite the school.

There was one old bay mare named Nellie who used to climb the hill every day just as school was being dismissed and she religiously left a pile in front of his gate. We used to watch for the ceremony and were never disappointed.

Nellie would begin to twitch her tail at the bottom of Donegal's property line; then she'd let out a monstrous fart or two; then her sides would begin to heave; her tail would be hoisted high and out of that collapsing rose of a hind end would cascade the aromatic nuggets of the day. Some said Nellie was the reincarnation of some poor teacher that Old Man Donegal had bedeviled to death. Anyway, we had plenty of ammunition!

That afternoon we gathered bags of horse turds: old ones, new ones, big ones and little. Our sidewalks had never been so clean, but only because all the horse manure was gone. The big, round, soup-plate-like mementos left by the cows were still everywhere. We called them cow-pasties.

We Uptowners were still assembling when the Frogs attacked. They had outflanked us, coming from the side road by the Methodist Episcopal Church, which wasn't fair. They gave us quite a trimming at first and those horse turds hurt like the devil when you got one in the ribs or the side of the neck. But the French and Indian kids spent their ammunition too hastily and ran short, whereupon the tide of battle shifted as our runners brought up new bagsfull. Then they overran our position and stole a lot of our turds. It was a real melee with about 40 kids from 9 to 14 taking part in the frenzy; crying laughing and screaming.

A new tactic suddenly appeared.

Someone got a stick, put it in one of the cow-pasties and flung the soft manure at his opponent with a most satisfactory result. Splat! You could see where the brown stuff hit and clung. In an instant, all of us were using sticks and slinging cow manure. Moments later, the sticks were forgotten and we grapped up handfuls of the crap and flung it. Oh, what a mess. Someone slammed a whole round saucer against the side of my face and I could only see out of one eye. It was one of my own comrades who had mistaken me for the enemy in the growing darkness. I gave him a fat handful right in the kisser! In moments all thought of sides was forgotten. We fought anyone near enough to be a target.

That was when Old Blue Balls Donegal made an error in judgment. He was suddenly in our midst, roaring and bellowing, knocking heads together and commanding us, in that terrible voice of his, to stop instantly and go home. A great juicy chunk of cow manure suddenly came from nowhere. It flew through the air and hit him square on the nose. Oh, what a noble splatter!

109

Our fighting stopped and all of us attacked Donegal. The air was literally full of cow-pasties and he was the one and only target.

He couldn't take it. He fled and we chased him, screaming with joy, down the street and right to his gate. We hugged each other; Uptowner, Downtowner, Finn, French and Indian. We danced and hurled epithets - and anything else we could find - at his house. It was a noble moment in all our lives... We never fought each other again.

OMNIUM AUREUM

Every two or three years nowadays, my wife, The Madam, fixes me with a steady brown eye and lays down an ultimatum: "Clean out your study or I will. It's throwaway time."

I can't blame her. I have to admit that the place is a disgrace with the piles of books teetering on the desk, stacked on the floor in the corners and all those papers, helterskelter everywhere. I even get a bit overwhelmed by the clutter at times - So, a few hours ago I got some cartons around and began discarding ruthlessly. I made some real headway too, until I found that old copy of Virgil's 'Aeneid' that my dad had given to Old Man Coon 50 years ago.

Coon was an old hermit who'd spent most of his life trying to find gold and had a mine of sorts up there on the headwatres of the Tioga. The old book's leather binding was ragged and broken and it still showed the tooth marks of the porcupine that had chewed it after the old man died. There was no point in keeping it, but I glanced through the pages briefly before throwing it away.

Inside the cover, in my father's Spencerian hand, was his name and the date, June, 1910, but what grabbed my attention was a slip of paper tucked tight into the final few pages.

On it was written, "Amicus medicus. Morturite Salutamus. Omnium aureum est in urnae tres divisa. In aqua sed non in fluvia." And it was signed, "H. J. Coon, March 14, 1918."

I haven't been able to think about anything else since I discovered that slip so I'd better put everything down on paper that I can remember about the circumstances while the memories are fresh in my mind. It's been over 50 years since Old Man Coon died.

H.J. Coon was always a mysterious figure. He wore his hair long, way below his shoulders, carried a pistol in his belt and came to town only twice a year, in September and May. Annie, the postmistress, said that there was always a registered letter waiting for him and he signed for it without comment and left. Then he took the train to Marquette, returned, bought a pile of groceries and a three gallon jug of whiskey, had a long sauna at Lahti's and went back into the woods.

My father said he was probably a remittance man, some black sheep

111

from a wealthy family out east, who they paid to stay away, far away.

Dad probably knew Mr. Coon better than anyone else in town because they shared the same curious hobby. They both had an interest in Latin literature.

As I've mentioned before, my father was a country doctor in a wilderness land, one of the few persons with any education thereabouts. His interest in Latin stemmed, he said, from the eight years of the language he'd taken in high school and medical school. He knew it well enough to be able to use some phrases when he talked with the Catholic priest and he often liked to make some comment in Latin when he was treating his patients. He said it helped in the healing process, that 90% of all medicine was humbug anyway and that a little incantation was almost as good as calomel or castor oil. Anyway, most of the townspeople were impressed by his learning and they had great faith in his medical skill.

Once, when Mr. Coon had come to town with a great boil on his neck, Dad, in the course of lancing it, had uttered some ancient Roman proverb, whereupon the old hermit capped it with another, also in Latin, much to dad's surprise and delight. He said that they then had a hell of a good conversation and that Mr. Coon was really a highly educated man. Dad thereafter insisted upon his having dinner with us whenever he came to town - hopefully only after he'd had his sauna and gotten rid of the half-year camp stink.

I don't remember much of what they talked about at the table - mostly philosophy and stuff, but never about gold - and they were always quoting things in Latin to each other.

Old Man Coon would never talk to anyone but dad, though, during those meals. He completely ignored my mother's attempts to engage him in conversation. She didn't like being shut out of the table talk and dreaded his bi-annual visits even though she had to admit that he had excellent table manners even if he wasn't polite to her. Anyway, on what was to be his last visit, my father gave Mr. Coon one of his two copies of Virgil. He said it should help him make it through the winter.

It didn't do it. Half way through February, the cruelest month of the north country winter, a timber cruiser for the Silverthorne Land Company had dropped in at the old man's cabin for a cup of java before snowshoeing the rest of the way back to town. He'd found the old hermit very weak from starvation. He'd been living for almost a month on oatmeal and buckfoot soup, made from deer hooves and horns. The timber cruiser told dad that a bear had broken into Coon's shack in late November and had just about cleaned the old man out except for one deer which he'd shot shortly afterward and on which he'd been living ever since. He said the old man was in bad shape.

Well, dad went right down to the store of course, and bought a good bunch of vittles - a bacon slab, beans, flour, tea, sugar and the like, maybe 40-50 pounds - enough to bulge a packsack to its seams anyway. But he had a terrible time trying to get someone to lug it up to Coon's homestead. Dad tried everywhere, threatened and begged, but no go. He said to my mother that he really couldn't blame them for refusing: 16 miles, four feet of snow on the level and no crust, rough country in that granite, 18 below zero at noon. It would be a bitter journey all right, but a man's life was at stake so dad, true to form, decided to go himself. When Jim Olson, caretaker of the mine property, heard he was going, he said he'd go along too, but at the very last minute dad had had to hop the caboose of the noon train. A woman up at Sidnaw had been in labor for two days and the baby was stuck crosswise, according to the telegraph message. So dad took off his hunting clothes, grabbed his black satchel and caught the train. He gave Jim Olson a ten dollar bill to hire someone to carry the provisions up to Old Man Coon. That was a heap of money in those days.

Anyway, everything got all fouled up and I forget how, but they let this half-breed, Will Twofeather, out of the village pokey where he'd been sobering up from a two-week bender, gave him dad's money, loaded him up with the groceries and put him on snowshoes headed for Coon's place. When dad finally returned from the Sidnaw confinement and they told him what they'd done, he was furious.

"Why the hell did you give that Indian bum the money first?" he hollered. "I'll bet he's over in a Nestoria saloon right now drinking it up. You never give an Indian any money until the job's done!"

Wow! Was dad ever mad. He was even biting his lower lip again. He stormed at the handful of men he had summoned.

"Damn the whole cowardly pack of you. Just wait till you get sick and call me next time. I'll cut the black gizzard right out of your guts and give you a taste of the stuff in the black bottle on the top shelf!"

Though they all agreed, the men didn't go that day or all the rest of the week because we got clobbered by a terrible blizzard with high winds and deep cold. It was reported that someone had seen Will Twofeather getting in an empty boxcar on the 7:29 train for the Soo or points east.

All that time dad kept worrying about Mr. Coon. When the blizzard finally ended, he got up another smaller box of groceries and hired three men, including One-Eye Foulin, to take it up to Coon's place, pulling the grub on a toboggan. They started at daybreak and returned about midnight that night. When they pounded on our back door, dad let them into the kitchen and made them a pot of coffee. I sneaked down the backstairs and hid behind the kitchen door so I could hear what they had to say.

"Yeah, we made it all right, Doc," said One-Eye Foulin. "Coon's dead. Frozen stiffer'n a preacher's prick. Was sittin' there in his rocking chair with a long log under his arm that come through a hole in the door. He had the other end stuck into the open door of the stove. Pretty slick idea, Doc. Thataway Old Coon don't carry any wood, just rock forward and nudge the log a bit more into the stove. But the fire was out, Doc, and there was Old Coon, just sittin'. He was friz so hard we couldn't unbend him no how. Just roped him onto the toboggan sitting up and drug him back that way."

The men said that it was kind of scarey sometimes, hauling him that way, what with him sitting back there like he was driving a team in the moonlight. They said One-Eye had given them a bad start when he suddenly grunted "Giddyap" and the others who were pulling thought it was the corpse that had spoken.

"Where'd you leave the body?" asked my father.

"Hell, he's right there by your back stoop, Doc. Take a look."

I ran back upstairs and saw the sight. There indeed was Old Man Coon sitting hunched up on that toboggan with the box of groceries between his legs. The ropes that held him ran around his body and then forward to the curve of the toboggan and they did look like reins. Pretty eerie! Old Man Coon, with his long hair, looked like a girl fixing to go on a sleigh ride. Scarey!

I returned to my eavesdropping behind the kitchen door.

"No. No sign of new groceries in the cabin, Doc. Everything bare as Tobey's butt. Nothin' to eat. The old man, he starved to death, for sure."

"Same as murder," my father said. "Take the body down to the depot and put him in the baggage room and tell the agent to ship it to the Ishpeming morgue as soon as he can. I don't want that hanging around here for the family to see in the morning. I'll make out a death certificate."

The men left, dad blew out the kerosene lamp and I heard the squeaky rasp of the toboggan as the men hauled Mr. Coon away - still driving the team.

That spring, about May break-up time, I got wind of an expedition my dad and Jim Olson were planning. They were going up to visit Old Man Coon's place. I wheedled and begged until they promised to let me come along. It was going to be pretty miserable they told me. We'd have to wade through icewater up to my neck in the flats. I'd have to carry my own blanket and food. Yes, and a fishpole too. There should be some early trout in the rapids. We might even have a chance to get into Old Coon's gold mine. I was so excited the night before we left that I couldn't sleep a wink.

It was a tough trip. Snow was still lying deep in the shadows of the north side of the hills and in the swamp pockets. That water in the flats flayed me with icy fire. I got soaked to the gills. Dad and Jim didn't walk slowly or wait for me at all. They just strode along up the endless trail while I had to run in spurts to keep them in sight. I remember thinking at times that I would try to make it to 'that birch tree' and then I'd die. I finally made it somehow, only to find them already in the cabin.

It was an unholy mess. The front door with the hole in it had been left ajar and the porkies had taken over. Dishes and pans were on the floor, chairs were overturned and gnawed and there were droppings everywhere on the floor, bed and table. An axe handle had been chewed almost through. A few books were squashed on the floor and they had torn pages.

Others had been there besides the porcupines.

"Look, Jim! They've already been up here hunting for the old man's gold," my dad said, pointing to a pile of earth on the floor.

When Jim pulled up the trap door we saw how someone had dug around the supports of the cabin beyond the confines of the square cellar, with its flattened, musty potato sacks. I was still shivering and shaking so much that the men told me to make a fire in the stove and sweep out the crap and corruption while they scouted around outside.

That's when I'd found the chewed copy of Virgil's 'Aeneid' with my dad's name in it, the one I'd just re-discovered this morning. I took it out to him as he was examining and explaining to Jim the operation of Coon's crude handmill for grinding up the quartz and greenstone ore.

"Yeah, that's the book I gave to H.J. last fall," he said. "What a mess. Stick it in the fire, Son. I've got a better copy at home."

But I put it in my pocket instead, along with a few chunks of ore as souvenirs. I wanted something to show the other kids to prove that I'd been all the way up to Coon's gold mine.

After supper I had some time to get outside and explore a bit myself. It was apparent that old Mr. Coon must have done a tremendous amount of work in the years of his hermitage. A four foot shaft had been sunk into the side of a solid granite bluff along a seam where the quartz gleamed white. I was scared to go into it. It was very dark and even I would have to bend my head. A grown man must have had it very hard, drilling and blasting and hauling rock in such a narrow shaft. There was also a large windlass made out of a hollow pine stub that Mr. Coon had set on a log frame. I could see that it could be turned by its large handles so he could pull up a bucket or ore or tailings from the shaft. I couldn't turn it myself.

What impressed me most was the hermit's rock pile. It ran for about 40 feet, out into the cedar swamp and it was almost seven feet high and about that wide. Every chunk in that causeway had been hewn or blasted out of solid rock. Surely Mr. Coon must have found something to have worked so hard.

I hunted for scraps of ore with yellow threads or pieces that were especially heavy. One chunk that I could hardly lift was full of little yellow cubes and I was sure I'd found some gold, but the men laughed when I lugged it to them excitedly.

"Fools gold! Iron pyrites," they said. "Not worth a damn. Look instead for little greenish threads in white quartz or yellow speckles on the green-gray stuff."

I didn't find any.

That night the men gave me the old man's bunk while they slept on some balsam branches by the stove. I fell asleep hearing them talk about gold and the men who sought it. They talked about the two real gold mines, the Ropes and the Michigan, both on this same formation of Old Man Coon's They'd taken more than a million dollars worth of gold out of each mine they said, but even more from the pockets of those who'd bought stock in them. No placer mining in this country. Any gold was always scattered in quartz veins and pockets. Dad told the tale of Bedford, the station agent at Clowry, who once got lost while trout fishing and how he cut cross-country to get home and found a chunk of quartz so rich it assayed $50,000 to the ton. And how Bedford spent the rest of his life hunting for the mother lode. He even hired him a prospector from out west one summer but never found it again. Jim told about the old shaft in the granite up there by Silver lake that no one knew anything about. The shaft was sealed people said, with an iron door. Jim had been there and it was true, he said. If Old Man Coon had been here for 30 years blasting and chunking and grinding, he must have found some gold and salted it away, they insisted. He had no heirs so far as they knew so now the land would probably go back to the state. Would it be worth buying at tax sale time? Hell no. Too hard to get in and out of in that kind of country. If old Coon had really got some gold and hidden it, where would he have put it? God, in all this forsaken country his cache would stay hidden forever. Maybe he left a will. We'll look for it in the morning. I fell asleep, listening to them talk.

In the morning, the men were drinking tea and eating hardtack when I awoke. They gave me a cup of it too, black as tar and with a coppery taste so strong I choked. Dad laughed and told me to go get a drink at the spring to take the fur off my tongue.

"You'll find it," he said. "Look for a square wooden box just to the left of the path leading to the creek. It's about halfway."

I found it easily, took off the square board lid and tried to get enough water by lapping it up with my cupped hands, but they leaked too much. I finally put my head down through the opening so I could drink directly. A precarious position, but while I was upside down there drinking, I noticed the tops of three jugs back behind the log framing of the spring. Curious, I tried to pull one out to see what was in it, but I couldn't budge it. Awfully heavy! It seemed to be anchored in stone. Oh well, who wants to lug home a heavy jug. I had another drink of water and forgot all about the jugs for 50 years. Until this morning cleaning my study, when I found what Old Man Coon had written on that yellow slip of paper in that copy of Virgil, the one I'd brought back as a boyish souvenir. "Amicus medicus." (Doctor, my friend.) "Moriturite Salutamus." (We who are about to die salute you.) "Omnium aureum est urnae tres divisa." (All the gold is divided into three urns.) Urns? Jugs! Three jugs in that spring! "In aqua." (In water.) "Sed in fluvia non est." (But not in the river.) In the spring! In the spring!.

I fear I must confess that I haven't made much progress in obeying The Madam's order. I keep looking at that old broken book and the yellow slip of paper. I keep remembering those three jugs in the spring. I keep wondering if I could possibly find a trace of Old Coon's mine again and its three urnae. I'm getting pretty old. There's no trail left up there. It's all grown over by now. Yet.....

"Northwoods Reader" artist Cindi L. Nowlen was born in the lake-shore city of St. Joseph, Michigan. She has received Bachelors of Science and Fine Arts degrees from Central Michigan University at Mt. Pleasant, Michigan while working as a graphic artist with the University for the past two years. It was at Central Michigan that she developed an interest in pursuing art as a profession.

Camping throughout Michigan has been a family experience for Cindi. "Never go in a straight line to anywhere," seemed to be the only rule of the road on those summer excursions and Cindi grew happily familiar with the natural bounty and people of her state.

This is Cindi's first solo book illustration effort. Her intuition, her feel for people and their emotions and her obvious skills with pencil and pen are certain to propel her on to many more such projects.

"I attempt to culture the versatile eye," says Cindi, "rather than capitalizing on the garish or the conventional. I want to create something intriguing to look at."

We at Avery Color Studios thank you for purchasing this book. We hope it has provided many hours of enjoyable reading.

Learn more about Michigan and the Great Lakes area through a broad range of titles that cover mining and logging days, early Indians and their legends, Great Lakes shipwrecks, Cully Gage's Northwoods Readers (full of laughter and occasional sadness), and full-color pictorials of days gone by and the natural beauty of this land.

Also available are beautiful full-color placemats and note stationery.

To obtain a free catalog, please call (800) 722-9925 in Michigan, or (906) 892-8251, or tear out this page and mail it to us. Please tape or staple the card and put a stamp on it.

PLEASE RETURN TO:

Avery Color Studios
Star Route - Box 275
Au Train, Michigan 49806
Phone: (906) 892-8251
IN MICHIGAN
CALL TOLL FREE
1-800-722-9925

Your complete shipping address:

_____

_____

_____

                                        _____

Fold, Staple, Affix Stamp and Mail

_____

_____

_____

          _____

Avery COLOR STUDIOS

Star Route - Box 275
AuTrain, Michigan 49806